PRAISE FOR THE JACK MASON ADVENTURES

'A fun stor
Bonus poi
its kind I'
    to the s

'Lots of me

breat........ ...... Michael Pryor

'Non-stop action, non-stop adventure,
non-stop fun!' Richard Harland

'Set in a fantastical London, filled with airships,
steam cars and metrotowers stretching into space,
this fast-paced adventure and homage to the world
of Victorian literature and Conan Doyle offers an
enjoyable roller-coaster read for fans of *Artemis
Fowl* and the Lemony Snicket series...[a] rollicking
who-dunnit that will keep young Sherlocks
guessing to the very end.' *Magpies*

'Charming, witty and intelligently written...
This series no doubt will be a huge hit for early
teens, the writing is intelligent and Darrell Pitt
has created characters that challenge and provoke
readers to invest in the storyline.' Diva Booknerd

THE JACK MASON ADVENTURES

Book I *The Firebird Mystery*
Book II *The Secret Abyss*
Book III *The Broken Sun*

DARRELL PITT began his lifelong appreciation of Victorian literature when he read the Sherlock Holmes stories as a child, quickly moving on to H. G. Wells and Jules Verne. This early reading led to a love of comics, science fiction and all things geeky. Darrell is now married with one daughter. He lives in Melbourne.

DARRELL PITT

The Broken Sun

A JACK MASON ADVENTURE

TEXT PUBLISHING MELBOURNE AUSTRALIA

textpublishing.com.au

The Text Publishing Company
Swann House
22 William Street
Melbourne Victoria 3000
Australia

First published in 2014 by The Text Publishing Company

Design by WH Chong
Cover illustration by Eamon O'Donoghue
Typeset by J&M Typesetting

Printed in Australia by Griffin Press, an Accredited ISO AS/NZS 14001:2004 Environmental Management System printer

National Library of Australia Cataloguing-in-Publication entry:
Author: Pitt, Darrell
Title: The broken sun: a Jack Mason adventure / by Darrell Pitt.
ISBN: 9781922182166 (paperback)
ISBN: 9781925095166 (ebook)
Target Audience: For young adults.
Subjects: Detective and mystery stories.
Dewey Number: A823.4

This book is printed on paper certified against the Forest Stewardship Council® Standards. Griffin Press holds FSC chain-of-custody certification SGS-COC-005088. FSC promotes environmentally responsible, socially beneficial and economically viable management of the world's forests.

This project has been assisted by the Commonwealth Government through the Australia Council, its arts funding and advisory body.

To Patrick
For leading the way

THE BROKEN SUN

CHAPTER ONE

'I need a seven-letter word that means *difficult to find*,' Scarlet Bell said, peering at the crossword puzzle in *The Times*.

'Hmm.' Jack Mason looked up from a book on mountain climbing. 'How about *exciting*?'

They were sitting in Ignatius Doyle's library on the top floor of 221 Bee Street. While it contained books—thousands of them—the shelves were empty. The books were stacked on the floor according to colour, while the shelves held odd items that had no place in a library: the chimney from a Stephenson steam engine, a fish tank containing a preserved snake, two stuffed monkeys, a jar marked 'Toenail Clippings', a vase with a bronze plate that read 'Ebenezer Jones—Much Loved but Easily Forgotten', a pile of men's undergarments and a cluster of oval spheres that looked like dinosaur eggs.

'I can see two problems with that answer,' Scarlet said, pushing back her fire engine red hair. 'The first is that *exciting* has eight letters.'

'Can't you just squeeze it in?'

At fourteen, Jack was a year younger than Scarlet, and small for his age. His expertise was not tests of the mind but the body. He and his parents had been trapeze artists in the circus. After their untimely deaths, he lived in an orphanage until Ignatius Doyle, the famous detective, employed him as his assistant.

'I've never heard of anyone doing that,' Scarlet said.

'What do the rules say?' Jack reached into one of the voluminous pockets of his green coat and withdrew a boiled lolly. 'I bet it's allowed.'

'There are no instructions saying you *can't* do it, but there is also a second problem. *Difficult to find* can hardly be defined as *exciting*.'

Jack wasn't so sure. Discovering the unknown with Mr Doyle often took them to exciting places. *Surely they are the same thing?*

Scarlet threw down the newspaper. 'We need a mystery to solve,' she said, giving up on the elusive word. 'I fear our brains are stagnating.'

Jack didn't mind a little stagnation. Their previous adventure had taken them all the way to America in the pursuit of the world's most deadly assassin. It was only through their efforts that a second civil war had been averted.

Wheeeeez.

Jack and Scarlet looked up. Mr Doyle's apartment contained several rooms with no ceilings. High above, leaky steam pipes and ventilation shafts crisscrossed the rafters. Nothing unusual there—except now a long metal wire was strung across the roof. Jack was sure it hadn't been there before.

A single pale feather seesawed lazily to the floor. The sound came again, and this time an enormous shape attached to the wire flashed overhead. Larger than a man, it had a beak and two great wings covered in white feathers.

'If I didn't know better,' Scarlet said, 'I'd say that was a giant seagull.'

'But that's impossible.'

'Which means Mr Doyle is conducting another of his little experiments.'

A crash came from the far end of the apartment.

'Oh dear,' Scarlet said. 'I think it may have failed.'

They followed the wire, weaving through more piles of odd possessions that clogged the apartment: a laboratory table covered in mouldy Petri dishes, a tank containing a rat skeleton, a model of the Eiffel Tower and a gorilla costume. They also passed Isaac Newton, the echidna. Sniffing the air, he disappeared through a curved hatch that had once been part of the Carlsdale Lighthouse.

3

Reaching a corner crowded with oversized chess pieces, a bust of Queen Victoria and a four-poster bed, Jack and Scarlet were just in time to see a birdman clambering off the mattress. The man shoved back a mask to reveal Mr Doyle.

'Fascinating,' he spat through a mouthful of feathers. 'I now believe the giant gull of Sumatra may have been a man in a costume suspended by a wire.'

'Ignatius Doyle! What on earth are you doing?'

Gloria Scott, the receptionist and live-in housekeeper, stormed into the room. She was tall with a mess of blonde ringlet curls and her kindly face was now creased into an expression of disbelief.

'Just conducting an experiment, my dear. Recent reports in the Malaysian press have told of a giant flying bird.'

'Are you sure it's not a bat? As in a belfry?'

The detective removed the outfit, reached into his long black coat and produced a piece of cheese. He popped it into his mouth. 'I don't know why you're so annoyed, my dear.' He smiled. 'Scientific experimentation lies at the heart of innovation.'

Gloria's face softened as she plucked a feather from Mr Doyle's ear. 'You are supposed to be setting an example for these young people,' she said. 'Children don't do as you say, they do as you do.' She pulled a letter from her pocket. 'Some mail arrived for you, Ignatius.'

'Mr Doyle?' said Jack when the detective examined the handwriting and frowned.

'I had best go to my study,' Mr Doyle murmured, the lines around his eyes appearing deeper than ever. 'I am feeling a little tired.' Without another word, he disappeared down an aisle, still clutching the letter.

'Gloria,' Jack said. 'What was all that about?'

She sighed. 'You'll have to ask Mr Doyle, but it's best to give him a few minutes.'

And without further explanation she too departed the room, leaving Jack and Scarlet to stare at each other.

'What on earth is going on?' Scarlet cried. 'I hope it's not bad news.'

Maybe it *was* bad news. 'Could someone have died?' Jack suggested. 'Possibly a friend?'

'I'm not sure Mr Doyle has any friends. Apart from us.'

Jack frowned. Mr Doyle did live a solitary life, immersed in solving crimes and carrying out strange experiments. And now that Jack thought of it, he had never seen him entertain a visitor not related to a case. 'We need to make sure he's all right,' he said.

They made their way through the apartment to the study door.

'Maybe this isn't such a good idea,' Scarlet said.

'Mr Doyle may need a friend. Who is that if it isn't us?'

Jack reached into his jacket, running his fingers over his two most prized possessions: the picture of him and his parents, and a compass. His mother and father had given them to him before their deaths, serving as a

5

reminder that he would never be alone.

No-one should be alone, Jack thought. *Especially when they need a friend.*

Jack knocked at the door.

'Come in,' Mr Doyle called.

Unlike the library, the study walls were covered in bookshelves filled with books. So many, in fact, that they overflowed onto the floor, with others teetering precariously on the desk. Nestled behind the books was Mr Doyle, wearing a pair of magnifying goggles. He was examining the letter.

'Mr Doyle. Is everything all right?'

'We were worried,' Scarlet added.

Removing the goggles, the detective offered them a seat.

'We didn't mean to pry,' Scarlet continued. 'But you looked a little upset.'

'Possibly more surprised than upset.' Mr Doyle slid the letter across the desk. 'Take a look at this.'

Jack and Scarlet began to read.

Dear Ignatius,

I know we have not spoken for some time, but a mystery has arisen concerning Phillip and I require your assistance. I would not have broken my silence with you unless I felt this matter to be of the utmost importance.

Yours,
Amelia.

Jack frowned. The names were familiar, but where did he know them from?

Scarlet said, 'Amelia is…?'

'My daughter-in-law. I have not seen her for many years.'

Now Jack remembered the story. Mr Doyle and his son Phillip had been in the war in France. It had been a terrible time with thousands of men dying in battle every day. After being ordered to attack an enemy emplacement, Mr Doyle and his men had charged across a field, but the detective had become entangled in barbed wire. Artillery fired upon them and, struggling to free himself, Mr Doyle had been knocked unconscious.

On waking, he searched for his son and the other men for hours, but it seemed they had all been killed. The only remains of Phillip Doyle had been his dog tags and some scraps of clothing. Nothing else was recovered.

Phillip's wife, Amelia, had been distraught. Blaming Mr Doyle for the loss of her husband, she had driven him away, forbidding him from seeing her or his grandson, Jason.

'A mystery concerning Phillip,' Jack said. 'I wonder what she means.'

'I have no idea,' Mr Doyle said. 'But I may be away for some time.'

'Then you will need our assistance,' Scarlet said.

Ignatius Doyle grimaced. 'I'm not sure how Amelia will receive us. She may be…difficult.'

Jack gave him a reassuring smile. 'Difficult, we can handle.'

Mr Doyle sent a message to his daughter-in-law informing her of his intended visit. The next morning Jack, Scarlet and Mr Doyle rose early, had breakfast and took the train to Harwich, a small town on the east coast. Mr Doyle's airship, the *Lion's Mane*, was still in repair after damage during their recent adventures.

The journey to Harwich took most of the day. It was a comfortable train, powered by a Vincent 700 steam locomotive. The engine was a mighty barrel-shaped chamber with a six-foot stack. Watching the smoke flow back towards the city, Jack's eyes were drawn to the London Metrotower, a crowning achievement of British engineering, reaching to the edge of space. From the top, steam-powered crafts transported people and goods between cities all around the world.

The invention of Terrafirma—a type of mould many times stronger than steel—meant that buildings could be constructed to enormous heights. The new Art Museum, Buckingham Palace and Houses of Parliament were over two hundred stories.

Scarlet nudged Jack. 'Have I shown you this?' she asked, waving a book at him. 'I'm sure you'll find it fascinating.'

Jack sighed. Their tutor, Miss Bloxley, gave them lessons five days a week. The woman had the special knack of making an interesting subject boring and a boring subject, well, very boring. In addition to this,

Scarlet had taken it upon herself to continue his education.

Jack read the cover: *The World of Classical Music.*

Oh no, he thought.

'That's right,' Scarlet grinned. 'More classical music.'

She proceeded to tell Jack all about Ludwig van Beethoven. Jack tried to appear interested but tuned out, only returning to the thread of the monologue when Scarlet described how Beethoven had gone deaf.

'I see,' Jack said. 'That explains a lot.'

'What do you mean?'

'All that banging about. Hitting things. It sounds like the orchestra is trying to kill a rat with their instruments.'

'You're saying that Beethoven's Ninth Symphony sounds like someone trying to kill a rat with a musical instrument?'

Scarlet had gone very pink. Jack swallowed. 'Maybe some of the girls at the music halls could help him,' he suggested. 'Teach him some songs.'

'The girls at the music halls? Beethoven could learn from *them*?'

'He can read lips,' Jack said. 'Can't he?'

'He's been dead for a hundred years.'

'Then lip reading's out of the question.' Jack flicked through the book. He liked reading, but adventure stories by writers such as Robert Louis Stevenson or Jules Verne. 'I'm not sure I know the meanings of all the words.'

'Which ones?'

'I can work out some of them,' Jack said.

9

'*Cat-as-trophe*. Imagine that, using a cat as a trophy. Should be a law against it.'

Mr Doyle coughed, covering a smile as Scarlet glared at Jack. 'Sometimes I think you say these things to annoy me,' she said.

'As if I'd do that.'

Arriving at Harwich Station, they found no steam-cabs so they walked the mile or so to Amelia's house. It was late in the day and the sky was clear of cloud. Jack breathed in the warm air. Spring had always been his favourite season because his mother had collected primroses, daffodils and snowdrops to decorate their small caravan.

'I have not been here in some time,' Mr Doyle said as they made their way down a lane lined with elm trees. 'Not since the war.'

'Has the area changed much?'

'Not at all. This has always been a quiet part of the country.'

'What sort of work did Phillip do?' asked Scarlet. 'Before the war.'

'He was studying medicine at Oxford. He never finished his studies or he would have entered as a doctor.' The detective sighed. 'I did not approve of his enlistment.'

'He enlisted?' Scarlet asked. 'I thought he must have been drafted.'

'A lot of men enlisted. They wanted to do their duty.' Mr Doyle did not speak for some time. 'War sounds so noble when you're seated around a living room with friends. The fire is blazing and the scotch is flowing. It's quite a different matter when you're in the middle of it.' He pointed. 'That's Amelia's house at the end.'

The neat two-storey brick cottage was surrounded by a hedge. They followed the path to a front door. Before Mr Doyle had a chance to knock, the door creaked open and a young woman appeared. Her black hair was pulled into a bun and there were dark shadows beneath her eyes.

'Amelia.' The detective smiled. 'It's lovely to see you.'

'Ignatius.' Her eyes shifted to Jack and Scarlet. 'Who are these young people?'

Once Mr Doyle introduced them, the woman's eyes blazed.

'And are you going to get them killed too?' she cried.

CHAPTER TWO

Amelia led them into a parlour. It was clean and tidy with walls covered in a floral pattern. There was an ornately carved bookcase in one corner and a faded olive-green lounge setting in the other. A vase of daisies sat on a sideboard, but the flowers were dry and wilted. Thin shards of sunlight came through the open curtains. A spider worked at a web in the corner of one window.

Jack felt uncomfortable as they sat on the lounge. The house was strangely quiet. Amelia sat like a tightly wound clock, her hands clenched together. Jack wished he and Scarlet had not come.

Over the fireplace hung a painting of a young man.

There was no mistaking his identity—Phillip Doyle looked just like his father.

'Is Jason here?' Mr Doyle asked.

'He is at school.'

Disappointment flashed across the detective's face. 'Then we might as well get to the heart of the matter,' he said. 'I assume someone has sent you Phillip's watch.'

Amelia's mouth dropped. 'How did you—?' She stopped herself. 'Of course. It is one of your little tricks.'

'The science of deduction is not a trick,' Mr Doyle said gently. 'I note the magnifying glass on the mantelpiece beneath the painting of Phillip. He is wearing the watch in the painting.' Mr Doyle pointed. 'I can only assume the bulky package next to the magnifying glass contains the watch.'

'It *is* his watch. It arrived three days ago. I didn't know what to do, but then I thought of you.'

'May I see it?'

She handed Mr Doyle the envelope. He peered inside, then removed a fob watch, a bronze device with an ivory face and gold hands.

'Was there a note?'

Amelia shook her head.

'Has anyone else other than yourself handled the watch or the envelope?'

'Only me.'

Mr Doyle produced his goggles and scrutinised the watch, before again turning his attention to the envelope.

'Do your powers tell you anything?' Amelia's voice

rose a notch. 'Or should your travelling circus move on to the next town?'

Jack could hold his tongue no longer. 'You should not be so rude to Mr Doyle,' he said. 'He is here to help.'

'Jack…' Scarlet warned.

'You don't know him,' Amelia said, gazing sadly at the portrait hanging over the fireplace. 'Not as I do.'

'I know you're angry with me,' Mr Doyle said, removing the goggles. 'But anger can destroy a person as surely as any disease.'

'He should never have gone to that terrible war.'

'You must focus on the future, Amelia.'

'What future?'

'Jason. *His* future.'

'I do.' Amelia gathered herself with a deep breath. 'He is all I have had—till now.'

Mr Doyle handed back the envelope. 'You asked if I was able to find any clues as to who may have sent this. This letter was sent by an elderly woman. She is left-handed and suffers from arthritis. Her hair is dyed blonde.'

Amelia looked amazed. 'That's…astonishing.'

'The envelope has a variety of scents,' Mr Doyle said. 'The first is a hand cream favoured by women of more advanced age. The second is a sharper scent. Hydrogen peroxide. Used to dye hair.

'The handwriting is that of a female. That she is left-handed is obvious from the slope of the script. She clearly suffers from arthritis. You see how'—he pointed to the letter—'she moves from one word to the next. There is a small line at the end of each, where she had difficulty lifting the pen. Still, the writing is otherwise legible and educated.'

'What about the watch?' Scarlet inquired.

'This *is* Phillip's watch,' Mr Doyle confirmed, picking up the timepiece. 'Not only does it carry the inscription I had engraved on the back, but it also has a tiny dent on the bottom right-hand side. This happened on a hiking holiday in Scotland.

'Two repairs have been made. The first is the hunter case. That is the spring-operated cover. It appears some damage was done to the spring and it has been replaced. A change has also been made to the back. This watch was an antique passed down from my grandfather,' Mr Doyle explained. 'It had a keyhole set into the back so that the spring could be wound. But if you look here,' he said, pointing at the case. 'It has been replaced with a winding stem. Only an experienced watchmaker could make such an alteration.'

'But you know what this means,' Amelia cried, leaping to her feet. 'You abandoned him to die on that battlefield, but he survived against all odds. Phillip is alive!'

Alive? Jack's mouth fell open. *Was it possible?*

'We can't jump to conclusions—' Mr Doyle said, but his face had turned very pale.

Scarlet leaned forward. 'Mrs Doyle,' she said. 'I understand your pain, but you must try to calm down.'

'How can I calm down?' Amelia was now brushing tears from her face. 'My husband has returned from the dead. I must find him!'

'I know losing Phillip has been difficult for you,' Mr Doyle said. 'Not an *hour* goes by that I don't think of him.'

'This house is so quiet without him.' Amelia stared behind them as if peering into the past. 'It is as though all the joy has been drained from it.'

'And Jason?' Mr Doyle asked.

'He is resilient,' Amelia said. 'Like his father.'

Mr Doyle swallowed. 'Is it possible for me to see him?'

'I don't think that would be wise. Not yet, anyway.'

'I understand,' the detective said, sighing. 'It's probably best that we move on. It appears we have a mystery to solve.'

'Who do you think sent me the watch?'

'There would be no mystery if I knew that answer.' Mr Doyle pocketed the watch and envelope, and they made their way to the front door. 'I will let you know what I discover.'

Amelia gulped. 'I must know the truth about my husband,' she said. 'Whatever that truth may be.'

Mr Doyle paused. 'Amelia,' he said. 'I am sorry.'

'I know.' She looked into his face as though seeing it for the first time. 'I also know you're the one person who can solve this mystery.'

They started back down the lane towards town.

Mr Doyle turned to Jack and Scarlet, his face bleak. 'I searched that battlefield for hours,' he said. 'Is it possible I missed something? Could Phillip still be alive?'

'As you said yourself, Mr Doyle,' Scarlet murmured, 'we can't jump to conclusions.'

'You're right. The most likely explanation would seem to be that someone found Phillip's watch on the battlefield and returned it to Amelia.'

'That makes sense,' Jack said.

'I suppose there is a chance—albeit a small one—that Phillip is alive.'

'May I see the watch, sir?'

Mr Doyle handed it to Jack. It was beautiful, quite old, but in excellent condition. The inscription on the back was delicately lettered:

To Phillip
Happy Eighteenth Birthday
Father

Jack felt his eyes sting. *Poor Mr Doyle, not knowing that Phillip would be killed in the war just a few years later.* And this after Mr Doyle had already lost his wife to cholera. Jack had always thought of the detective as a brilliant and eccentric man. It was strange to think of him as a family man. His life would have been quite different if he had not lost his wife and son.

It made Jack realise how things would have been for him too. The great detective had completely changed

Jack's life since removing him from the orphanage.

Mr Doyle sighed as he took a piece of cheese from his pocket and chewed on it.

'What are you thinking?' Jack asked.

Mr Doyle swallowed. 'I was remembering when Phillip was a boy,' he said. 'There was a song I used to sing to him. An old Irish song.' He cleared his throat and softly sang:

> *The Minstrel Boy will return we pray*
> *When we hear the news we all will cheer it,*
> *The Minstrel Boy will return one day,*
> *Torn perhaps in body, not in spirit.*

They soon reached the town. It was late, so Mr Doyle suggested they stay overnight. They found a small thirteenth-century hotel called The Goose and Duck, a tidy establishment with low doors and small windows that overlooked the surrounding countryside.

The next morning they rose early, ate a hearty breakfast and readied themselves for the day ahead.

'Where to, Mr Doyle?' Scarlet asked.

'The postmark of the letter is Southwold.'

'Isn't that on the coast?' Jack asked.

'It's north of here. We'll take a steamer.'

They travelled by train to the coast and boarded a steamer called the *Darbishire*, a sardine-shaped vessel covered in bronze plating with two paddle wheels at the back. It could hold a hundred people, but it was a quiet day with only a few dozen on board.

Jack and Scarlet left Mr Doyle inside, went out onto the deck and gazed out to sea. The air was fresh on Jack's face as he leaned against the railing.

'There's a Brinkie Buckeridge book just like this,' Scarlet said. '*The Adventure of the Missing Ear.* It begins innocently enough when Brinkie loses her best shoes. It turns out they were stolen by her evil twin sister.'

'I didn't know she had a sister,' Jack said.

'Neither did she,' Scarlet said, lowering her voice conspiratorially. 'It seems Lavinia Buckeridge was taken away at birth and raised by a Russian spy family in America. Brinkie is kidnapped and Lavinia takes her place. She is only discovered through the efforts of Wilbur Dusseldorf, Brinkie's lover *and* nemesis. He realises that Brinkie and Lavinia are identical in every way, except Lavinia has a freckle on her left elbow.'

'Lucky,' Jack sighed.

Scarlet nodded enthusiastically. 'It is only Lavinia's inherent goodness that makes her renounce her evil ways. Both she and Wilbur unite to save Brinkie from certain death.'

'Hmm,' said Jack.

'Brinkie also has a brother. He's another story, but he too was taken away at birth.'

'So Brinkie is one of triplets?'

'Quadruplets, actually.'

'Blimey!'

If only mysteries could be solved as easily as they are

in books, Jack thought. Mr Doyle was usually upbeat at the start of an investigation, but he had been unusually quiet this time. *Shouldn't he be excited to learn his son could still be alive?*

'Sometimes not knowing is worse than knowing,' Scarlet mused. 'You remember when we first met, my father went missing. Those were some of the most difficult days of my life. Not knowing if he was alive or dead.'

Scarlet's father, Joseph Bell, was now designing a metrotower in China. Jack thought about his parents. He tried to imagine what it would feel like if someone told him they were alive, and he was surprised to find it a disconcerting thought. He pulled out his compass.

'You must think about your parents a lot,' Scarlet said.

'Every day.'

'My mother died when I was very young, so I never knew her. I often wonder what she was like.'

'Probably like you,' Jack said.

'Witty, beautiful and destined to become Britain's first female prime minister?'

Scarlet was a firm supporter of women's rights. She was convinced that women would one day share the same rights as men, including the right to vote and even hold political office.

'I'm sure,' Jack said. 'Let's go in. I want to make certain Mr Doyle is all right.'

Inside, they found their mentor sitting next to a window, staring through the glass with unfocused eyes.

'Is everything all right?' Jack asked.

Mr Doyle nodded. 'I'm afraid I'm rather distracted. I keep thinking back to that day on the battlefield.'

Scarlet gripped his shoulder. 'You did everything you could.'

Mr Doyle gave them a wan smile. 'I always wonder if I should have done more. If there was something I missed,' he said. 'I do believe we're almost there.'

The steamer was now slowing as it pulled in towards the coast. It docked at a large port and they disembarked with a small group of other travellers. Scarlet's eyes narrowed as she examined the village. 'What an interesting town,' she said. '*Very* interesting.'

'What do you mean?' Jack groaned.

White terrace houses with slate roofs packed the narrow streets, bay windows jutting onto footpaths. An old brown mare dragged a milk cart past a fisherman on an upturned bucket, his line trailing in the water. A squat lighthouse nestled among houses a street back from the sandy beach. Brightly painted bathing boxes faced the water.

'It just looks like a normal seaside town to me.'

'Exactly,' Scarlet said. 'Too normal.'

'How can something be too normal?'

Scarlet turned to Mr Doyle for support and the detective thought for a moment.

'Certainly it is common to seek out things that stand out from the ordinary,' he said. 'But sometimes things can seem *too* ordinary. I once investigated a string of robberies committed by a man known as the Shadow. When I plotted the thefts on a map, I discovered them to be exactly half a mile away from each other.'

Jack couldn't see anything wrong in this. 'So why was that strange?'

'Serial criminals always begin by committing crimes in an area close to home. The Shadow was desperate to hide his point of origin, so desperate in fact that it meant he lived very close to the first robbery. I checked with the police as to known offenders in the area and he was arrested the same day.'

Scarlet beamed. 'Brinkie works the same way,' she said. 'I will keep an eye out for extraordinarily normal behaviour.'

'So will I,' Jack said. 'Let's arrest anyone who looks too normal and sit on them until the police arrive.'

'You're being silly.'

'No, seriously,' Jack said. 'You see that old lady?' A frail-looking woman had just come out her front door. 'She looks far too much like an innocent old lady. She might be a werewolf. Or a leprechaun. Maybe even a sea monster. We *are* near the ocean, after all.'

Scarlet ignored him. 'I believe I will develop a theory,' she said. 'I will call it the *Theory of Normal Strangeness*.'

'That's got quite a ring to it. Your friend, Mr Beethoven, might be able to turn it into a song.'

'Sometimes I want to hit you.'

Mr Doyle intervened before violence could ensue.

'We should first find accommodation,' he said, glancing at his watch. 'It's almost midday. We'll eat and then unravel this mystery one thread at a time. Werewolves or no werewolves.'

Jack and Scarlet were pleased to see Mr Doyle had recovered some of his good humour. They booked a room in a hotel called The Belvedere, eating a meal of steak-and-kidney pies while Mr Doyle engaged the waitress in idle conversation. Around twenty, the young woman was slim, reminding Jack of a greyhound, and she was more than happy to respond to queries about the town.

'A few businesses have closed,' she explained. 'These seaside places have a boom and bust economy. It's spring now and we're doing all right, but it's quite slow in winter.'

'I am in need of a watchmaker,' Mr Doyle said. 'Is there one nearby?'

'There was one, but he closed years ago.'

'There's no-one who can do repair work?'

She thought for a moment. 'A group of people have moved into the old Westlake House on the south road. I think they're some kind of engineers.'

'Really?'

She leaned close. 'Lots of equipment gets delivered to the home. A box got broken at the station and some gear spilled out. One of the men was furious.'

Mr Doyle rubbed his chin, looking thoughtful. He confirmed the address and thanked the waitress. She left them to finish their meal.

'Did you see that?' Jack asked Scarlet. 'That girl was so much like a waitress that she was *too* much like a waitress. What do you think, Mr Doyle?'

The detective produced a lump of cheese from his pocket. He had the strangest eating habits of anyone Jack knew.

'She is behaving very much like a waitress,' he said, 'because she *is* a waitress. Her parents own the establishment and she is getting married next year. Which will be nice because the cat she owned for seven years recently died.'

Jack and Scarlet looked at each other and laughed.

After leaving the pub, Mr Doyle hailed a steamcab, directing the driver to a large property surrounded by a high stone wall and overhanging trees. Foliage hid the house beyond. When Mr Doyle paid the driver they all climbed out of the cab.

'There has been some movement here, but not in the last week.' Mr Doyle pointed at the driveway. 'Recent tyre tracks.'

He went to climb over the gate when Scarlet asked, 'Isn't that trespassing?'

'Not at all. We've simply lost our way.'

The metal gate had spikes running across the top. Jack and Mr Doyle navigated them without difficulty, but Scarlet was momentarily ensnared by her dress. At the end of the driveway was a two-storey Georgian home with a well-maintained garden. Mr Doyle knocked at the front door. No-one answered.

'Should we break in?' Jack asked.

Mr Doyle gave a gentle laugh. 'Breaking and entering is a crime,' he reminded his young assistant. 'And we never break in.'

'Sorry?'

'But we do occasionally enable an entry point. Let's look around.'

They found an empty sunroom at the back. The windows were dusty and locked. Mr Doyle knocked again, but there was still no answer. Scarlet glanced through another window.

'That's the kitchen,' she said. 'There are tables and chairs, but no pots or pans.'

'Really?' Mr Doyle said. 'That's odd.' He peered in. 'Hmm. No plates. No dishes. No sign of habitation. You know what that means?'

'What?'

'That the time has come to enable an entry point.' He raised his elbow and knocked it against the glass, smashing it out of the pane. Reaching inside, he undid the latch.

'What will we say if someone *is* inside?' Scarlet asked.

'We'll tell them we're lost,' Mr Doyle said, 'and seeking the road to Edinburgh.'

'I'll go,' Jack offered, starting to push the window open. But Mr Doyle suddenly threw himself at him.

'Watch out!'

CHAPTER THREE

They hit the ground and rolled as the window shattered, spraying glass and timber everywhere.

After a long moment of stunned silence, Mr Doyle calmly rose to his feet and inspected the opening. 'A rifle has been set as a booby trap. I saw it at the last moment.'

Jack stood, his legs shaking. He tried to speak, but his throat was still blocked with fear. He would have been killed if Mr Doyle hadn't pushed him out of the way.

'Are you all right, my boy?' Mr Doyle asked, gripping his shoulder.

'Fine,' Jack said, his voice an octave higher.

'At least we have an answer to one question: no-one else is here. They would have come running by now.'

Scarlet nodded. 'I should have realised that window was too normal.'

Jack wondered if there could really be something to her *Normal Strangeness* theory. 'Shame the house wasn't gloomy and mysterious,' he said. 'It might have been safer.'

Mr Doyle eased open the shattered window. Jack peered inside and saw that a rifle had been harnessed to a series of pulleys and levers, ready to fire when the window was opened.

Jack shuddered. 'Thank you, sir,' he said. 'You saved my life.'

'My pleasure.'

They searched the house. Grey curtains with a peacock design hung in each room, swathing them in dull light. The carpets were threadbare. Bald patches discoloured the walls where paintings had once been displayed. A nursery, brightly clad in royal blue wallpaper, was empty except for a solitary child's alphabet block in a corner. The house contained nothing of a personal nature. No pictures of family members. No crockery or cutlery. No papers or clothing.

Downstairs, other traps had been set under every window, as well as the front and back doors.

'This is possibly taking security a little too seriously.' Mr Doyle chewed on some cheese as he examined the front door. 'There is a piece of string here that deactivates the trap.'

Reaching a room lined with bookshelves without

books, Mr Doyle nodded in satisfaction. 'Ah,' he said. 'This is fortunate.'

'I already feel fortunate,' Jack said, 'to not have a hole in me.'

The detective pointed to the floor. 'You see how the dust has been disturbed. There was equipment in this room. I believe it was only recently removed.'

'So whoever sent the watch has left,' Scarlet said, 'and removed everything of importance?'

'I think so.' Mr Doyle inhaled deeply. 'There is a strange smell in the air.'

Jack and Scarlet breathed in. 'Could it be cleaning fluid?' Scarlet asked.

'I suspect they were doing more than engineering here.'

The next room was a windowless sitting room, containing a couple of chairs, a small side table and lamp. It was a murky chamber, the only light entering through the doorway.

Mr Doyle activated the gaslight and the interior brightened. Reaching into his pocket, he pulled out a small bust of Napoleon. 'Oh dear,' he said. 'I was wondering where that went.' Returning the bust, he dragged out his goggles and scanned the room. 'This is *very* odd. Why would someone construct such a dark, dingy room? It looks like it was once part of the library.'

Jack crouched. 'There's a line running across here,' he said. 'Actually, it looks like—'

But that was as far as he got as the trapdoor gave

way and Jack found himself falling through the air.

Thud!

Landing in a heap on the floor, he heard Scarlet and Mr Doyle cry out just as the trapdoor sprang back into place.

'Bazookas,' Jack groaned, rubbing his rump. 'Wasn't expecting that.'

He had landed in a wine cellar, an enormous chamber packed with dozens of long racks. Two aisles ran across the middle, with gaps at each end where the racks did not touch the edges. Light cut like shards of broken crystal from tiny windows set high in the walls. Cobwebs stretched across the ceiling, a startled spider racing away. Jack doubted anyone had been down here in years.

He wrinkled his nose. There was a strange smell about. A bad smell. *What was it? Rotting meat?*

Thudding came from above, and Scarlet and Mr Doyle's voices reverberated through the timber. Jack was about to shout back when something clattered on the far side of the cellar.

Something else is down here.

'Hello?' Jack asked. 'Is anyone there?'

Jack crossed the cellar, scanning for movement. Surely no-one lived down here. Unless they were a prisoner. Maybe the owner was keeping someone captive?

More movement at the far end of the aisle.

'Hello?' Jack ventured.

He was halfway down the aisle when the figure

29

moved into a shaft of light. Jack gasped. It wasn't a person at all. It was a bull, twice its normal size. Three sharp horns protruded from its forehead, and below these a huge jaw lined with fangs.

Jack froze. *How is this possible?*

The creature must be an illegal biological experiment. Were the Darwinist League responsible? They worked at the cutting edge of natural science, and much of their work was revered. They had created oak trees that grew in the shape of planks of wood, fish that lived on land and domesticated elephants the size of house cats. They were even engineering whales that could carry humans like submarines.

The creation of modified animals was strictly controlled, but some scientists carried out illegal experiments. This deformed bull appeared to be such a creature. The scientist who had created it had been far from successful: it had no eyes. Jack relaxed slightly. The beast was enormous, but Jack would be all right as long as he was quiet.

Taking a step backwards, Jack's feet scraped against the stonework. The bull lifted its head, sniffed the air and started down the aisle. Jack turned to run, but in his panic tripped and fell.

Move, a voice in his head screamed. *Move!*

Jack scrambled to his feet and dived into the next aisle. The bull ploughed past. *How can such an enormous beast run so fast?* Jack tore down the aisle, darting sideways again as it thundered by.

He could hear it sniffing and snorting, and then the bull emitted a roar like a deranged lion. Jack's blood ran cold. He scanned the gloom for an exit. Nothing. The walls were bare. There was no door.

But there has to be a way out of here!

He made for a break in the shelves halfway down the aisle as the beast made another pass, closer this time. It had slowed to a trot, roaring in frustration. With those teeth, it had to be a carnivore. Maybe it hadn't been fed in days. Or weeks...

I don't want to be its next meal.

Jack watched the bull reach the end of the aisle, before tiptoeing towards the far wall, praying he'd find a door in one of the murky corners. He quietly edged along, peering into the shadows.

Nothing.

The bull was silent and unmoving—for the moment. Jack glimpsed something hanging from the ceiling about twenty feet away. A thick strand of cobweb. *No*, he thought. *It's a length of rope.*

Could it be a handle for a set of pull-down stairs?

Jack crossed another aisle...

...and fetid breath snorted directly into his face.

A piece of advice from Mr Doyle floated into his mind like a bubble rising to the surface of a lake.

Your assumptions can kill you.

The great detective was correct. What on earth had made Jack think there was only *one* bull in the cellar?

The second bull grunted. It could smell him. Like its

brother, it had no eyes, but would be on Jack in a flash if he made the slightest sound. The monster's head weaved about in the air. Jack's scent was clearly driving it wild.

A sound came from the opposite end of the cellar. The other bull was getting closer. Jack imagined their reaction when they found him sandwiched between them.

Hello food!

Jack had to think fast.

Edging a hand into his pocket, he took out a coin and, clenching it tightly, raised his shaking arm. The bull sucked in another deep breath, and its three horns moved dangerously close to Jack's face.

Jack tossed the coin over the bull's head. It seemed to take an eternity to arc across the aisle before it hit the floor and bounced away. The beasts roared, charging after it. Jack ran towards the rope and, as if by magic, stairs folded down from the ceiling.

What the—?

Mr Doyle came down the steps.

'No!' Jack screamed. 'Run!'

He flew towards the stairs as something thudded behind him. A bull was only a few feet away. Jack charged up the steps and past the detective as the creature started clambering up.

'Good heavens!' Scarlet cried.

Mr Doyle still held the lamp in his hand. He threw it down at the monster's head, spreading flame and oil across its face.

'Go!' Mr Doyle yelled. 'Go!'

He pushed Jack and Scarlet out of the room, pulling the door shut just as the beast's horns smashed through the timber.

Then Jack was outside. *Free!* But even as Mr Doyle pulled the front door closed Jack could still hear the roar of the beasts—a rabid bellow, and the crash of falling objects as they charged from room to room.

'I think the building's on fire,' Mr Doyle said.

'I don't care if the whole world's on fire!' Jack said, still shaking. 'Just as long as we're away from those… things.'

Within minutes smoke was seeping from the eaves. They started towards town with the sound of breaking glass echoing after them. Jack looked back to see a column of smoke rising into the clear sky.

'Have you ever noticed how many buildings burn to the ground when we're around?' Mr Doyle asked.

'That happens to Brinkie all the time,' Scarlet replied. 'In *The Adventure of the Singing Book*, she is caught in a burning church, house, barn, rollerskating rink, opera house and factory that produces xylophones.'

'That makes me feel rather better, my dear,' Mr Doyle said. 'One might even say it's *music to my ears*.'

Jack and Scarlet groaned.

'How is that possible?' Jack asked Scarlet. 'No-one can have such bad luck.'

'Luck had nothing to do with it,' Scarlet said. 'It turned out that Brinkie's cousin, Abernathy Buckeridge, was a pyromaniac. He loved setting fires.'

'I love fires too—as long as they're in a fireplace.'

Another enormous crash came from the distant house. Part of the roof had collapsed. More smoke and burning embers flew up as a fire engine trundled over a distant hill, siren blaring.

'At least we can be certain of one thing,' Mr Doyle said. 'We're on the right track.'

By now it was late in the day. They returned to their hotel, packed their belongings and were shortly on a train travelling back to London. It seemed to Jack that weeks had passed since they left Bee Street.

Settling back into his seat, he leafed through the book that Scarlet had given him, opening to a section about Mozart.

'Now this is interesting,' he said.

'What is?' Scarlet asked.

'It says here that Mozart died at the age of thirty-five. Foul play was suspected. It looks like someone didn't like his music.'

'That seems most unlikely,' Scarlet objected.

'He's wearing a very funny wig in this picture,' Jack said. 'Maybe someone didn't like his hair.'

'That's hardly a reason for murder!'

Mr Doyle spoke up. 'Actually, people have been murdered for many strange reasons. Lovers' tiffs. Small-minded prejudices. Quarrels. I investigated a crime where a killer targeted women with messy hair.'

'Really?' Scarlet said, tidying her locks. 'Imagine that.'

Jack fell asleep, dreaming of bulls and roaring

monsters. He woke just as they pulled into Liverpool Street Station. The streets were dark, lit only by gaslamps. A fog had moved in, enveloping the streets.

After taking a horse-drawn buggy back to Bee Street, they found Gloria in the office, updating Mr Doyle's files. The detective had two dozen filing cabinets crammed into a coffin-shaped room in a corner of the apartment. Not only did he keep his case files, but he also tracked several other occurrences here: geese migration patterns, weather reports, the personal column from *The Times*, airship timetables, reports of circus accidents. The list went on. Jack had asked him why he kept an eye on such a strange assortment of things.

'You never know when such knowledge may come in handy,' Mr Doyle had responded mysteriously.

'Welcome back,' Gloria now said. 'Anything exciting to report?'

'Just the usual,' Scarlet said, grinning at Jack's look of incredulity.

After they freshened up, Jack and Scarlet returned to a meal of sausages and mash. While they ate, Mr Doyle picked at his food, thumbing through a book on the history of watchmaking.

Gloria raised her hand. 'Did you hear that?' she asked.

'What?'

She left the sitting room and returned a minute later with an envelope, handing it to Mr Doyle.

He unfolded the letter.

'Now this is interesting. A page of the calendar with next week marked through,' he said. 'And a place written across the page. Section Twelve of the British Museum.'

'What does it mean?' Jack asked.

'I don't know, but the handwriting is identical to that found on the envelope delivered to Amelia. I believe someone wants us to be at the museum next week. Section Twelve is the Ancient History department,' Mr Doyle mused. 'I wonder what is slated to happen.'

'Should we contact the police?'

'They won't do anything based on such flimsy information, but I think having eyes and ears on the inside may give us an advantage.'

'Who were you thinking of?' Jack asked.

The detective smiled. 'Who do you think?'

CHAPTER FOUR

'And I'm sure you recognise this as being from Ancient Rome,' Doctor Charles Benson said, smiling genially. 'What period does it come from, Jack? Take a stab.'

Jack peered at the bowl with feigned interest. He glanced at Scarlet, but she simply raised an eyebrow. Jack was certain she knew the answer—Scarlet knew the answer to everything—but refused to give him any clues.

The British Museum had changed over the past ten years. The original building had been remodelled and was now housed within a perfect bronze cube with a glass ceiling. It had so many rooms that even the staff sometimes got lost.

Jack and Scarlet had been assisting an old friend of

Mr Doyle's, Doctor Benson, in the research department. At first Jack had been excited, but his enthusiasm quickly faded: rather than learning about suits of armour and battles and Egyptian mummies, he had spent the week studying broken bowls, vases and pieces of pottery. When he offered to throw one in the bin, the panicked professor snatched it from him. It dated back to the second century BC, apparently.

'Can't you just buy a new one?' Jack had asked.

Not often did Jack doubt the abilities of Ignatius Doyle, but this time he was sure they were on the wrong track. Ancient History in the British Museum was enormous, covering hundreds of square feet. The research department, three floors below ground, contained pieces that had not yet been identified, or were too valuable for display.

The underground section resembled a railway station with pendant lights hanging from the ceiling, illuminating the grey tiled walls and stone floors. Mahogany work benches and walnut-veneered display cabinets, containing items still to be catalogued, clogged the rooms. Dozens of staff worked here at any one time, cataloguing acquisitions or determining their origin.

During the week, Jack and Scarlet kept an eye out for anything relating to the case—Darwinist experiments, missing men from the war, watches—but nothing appeared out of the ordinary. It was all remarkably normal.

'What period?' Jack now said, biting his lip. 'Could it be...the lunch period?'

'No! No, my boy!' Doctor Benson had bushy eyebrows that danced up and down when he got excited. 'Late Rome! Fourth century AD!'

'Yes, Jack,' Scarlet said, trying to stifle a grin. 'Fourth century. How could you not know that?'

Jack shot her a look that would have wilted daisies.

The doctor held up a hand. 'Possibly it's time for lunch. We'll delve further into the clays of the late Roman period when you return.'

'There must be many differences between early and late Roman clay,' Scarlet said, giving Jack a discreet wink.

'There are.' The doctor looked at her delightedly. 'We can spend the whole afternoon on them!'

Scarlet's face froze. 'Wonderful,' she said through her teeth. 'We look forward to it.'

They escaped, leaving the doctor to examine a tiny shard of Roman pottery that could have been mistaken for a rock.

'You are so terrible,' Jack said to Scarlet. 'You encourage him!'

'I'm conducting an experiment,' Scarlet said. 'Can you fall asleep while standing up?'

'Not only am I asleep, but my eyes are still open!'

'So that's why you were drooling.'

'I was not... I wasn't drooling. Was I?'

Scarlet laughed. They passed a table where an intern by the name of Matthew Pocket looked up. 'It's our young work-experience students,' he said. 'Not bored yet, are you?'

39

'Bored isn't really the word,' Jack said.

'Old Benson means well,' Pocket said. 'But he can talk the leg off a chair. You should take a walk around the Mesopotamian section. A new display is on show.'

It sounded like an interesting way to spend their lunch break. They thanked Matthew Pocket and went up in a wheezing elevator to the visitor's section. It was a quiet afternoon, with only a few people spread around the exhibit.

'I've often visited the museum with my father,' Scarlet said. 'It's changed a lot over the years.'

Mythical creatures, made from bronze, decorated the cornices of the rooms, with scenes from history painted on the ceilings. Even the tiled floors had historical facts inscribed across them. A person could glance down and discover the location of the Battle of Waterloo or the launch date of the world's first steam-powered spaceship.

The museum was one of the biggest purchasers of cut flowers in the country. Every visitors room contained a vase on a stand in the corner, giving the building a fresh perfumed smell. Classical music, channelled throughout the exhibits, added to the atmosphere.

One of Jack's favourite things at the British Museum was the life-size dioramas displaying ancient people in their historical surroundings. There were hundreds of them, set into the walls like stages in a theatre; moments of history frozen in time.

'That one looks like Miss Bloxley,' Jack said, pointing. He was amazed at the resemblance. Evolution and family inheritance had unfortunately made their tutor look rather frog-like. 'I didn't know she was alive in ancient times.'

'You mustn't be so horrible about Miss Bloxley. She's not that old. And she doesn't look like a frog. She looks like...well, she does look a *little* froggy.'

In the centre of the room were glass display cabinets, containing weapons, masks and more pieces of pottery. As Jack and Scarlet stopped at one, an elderly man with a beard and eyes like those of a basset hound crossed the floor, dragging a heavy bag on wheels. He looked about uncertainly.

When Scarlet offered him assistance, he shook his head.

'Thank you, young lady. I'm searching for the African section.'

'We can take you there,' Scarlet said.

'I've donated a number of pieces to the museum,' said the man as they walked to the next exhibit. 'The museum has been cataloguing them.'

'Have you been to Africa?' Jack asked.

'Certainly. I'm Professor James Clarke.' The way the man said it made Jack think he was supposed to know the name. 'I'm an archaeologist. I suppose you wouldn't know me if you're not interested in African artefacts.'

'I don't really know anything about them.'

'I didn't either when I was your age,' Professor Clarke said. 'Although I was a reader. My favourite book was *Ivanhoe* by Sir Walter Scott. Have you read it?'

'Yes, sir. I loved it.'

'And you, my dear?' The professor turned to Scarlet. 'Do you also like reading?'

Jack groaned. Scarlet shot him a look before regaling the old man with an outline of the Brinkie Buckeridge books.

Professor Clarke's bag looked very heavy. *One of us should help him with that*, Jack thought. As he reached for it, the professor grabbed his wrist. His grip was surprisingly strong.

'I'm fine. Thank you.' He released Jack. 'These items are quite valuable. They must not leave my care.'

They entered another section with dark-green walls and dioramas of life-size South American people. Professor Clarke crossed to a glass display in the centre of the room.

'This was purchased by the museum last year. It's the Cusco necklace, named for the ancient Inca city in which it was found.'

'It's amazing,' Scarlet said. 'Is that—'

'Gold? Yes. Legend has it that the necklace was once worn by the Emperor Kalamazar.'

It was an exquisite silver circle that fitted around the neck, and all the way around the outside were flat, lozenge-shaped bars made of gold.

'It must be very valuable,' Jack said.

'It is,' the professor said. 'I believe—'

A gunshot split the air. A woman screamed. Jack turned to see a family diving for cover. Two masked men were in the doorway, waving guns about. Dressed in blue trousers and jackets, they were wearing porcelain masks, one smiling, one frowning. They fired a second shot into the ceiling.

Professor Clarke abandoned his bag. 'Take cover!' he cried, shoving Jack and Scarlet behind a seat in the corner.

'Everyone on the floor!' one of the men yelled.

Jack heard the sound of glass smashing. Another bullet rang out. He peered around the seat.

'What's happening?' Scarlet asked him.

'They're singing a little song about butterflies! What do you think is happening? It's a robbery!'

Jack squinted. There was something strange about their outfits. What was it?

I know. Those are police uniforms, but without the insignia.

There was no doubt about it. They were either real police officers or…

The one wearing the smiling mask stared at Jack. Ducking away, Jack heard the sound of approaching footsteps before he was grasped by the back of his collar and had the cold barrel of a gun pressed against his head.

'I don't like people staring at me,' the man said.

'Leave him alone!' Scarlet cried.

The man's gun moved away from Jack. Scarlet gasped as it was pointed at her.

'Don't look at me!' the man snapped. 'Do it again and you'll be sorry!'

43

Jack was terrified. The man cuffed him across the head and swore. Scarlet gripped Jack's hand. The armed man retreated. Somewhere in the room a child started crying. A man tried to console a weeping woman.

Someone touched Jack's shoulder. He looked up to see Professor Clarke.

'They're gone,' the old man told him. 'And they've stolen the Cusco necklace!'

CHAPTER FIVE

Within an hour, the British Museum was flooded with police and emergency services in search of the thieves.

'Jack! Scarlet! Are you all right?'

Ignatius Doyle hurried towards them.

'Just a little shaken up,' Scarlet said.

'If you can call absolute terror *a little shaken up*,' Jack added.

Police interviewed witnesses. When the broken display case was thoroughly processed, a photographer took pictures with a square bellows camera the size of a bread bin, set up on a tripod.

Jack noticed Inspector Greystoke—an old friend of Mr Doyle's from Scotland Yard—enter the room.

The inspector arrowed over. 'Doyle!' he said. 'I should have expected you to be involved in this!'

'Only peripherally,' Mr Doyle said. 'It was my young assistants who were at the heart of the action.'

Greystoke asked them to go through the chain of events, and Jack and Scarlet obliged. They explained about meeting Professor Clarke and the arrival of the masked men. Mr Doyle listened thoughtfully while the inspector made notes on a small jotter.

'So you believe these men were dressed as police officers?' Greystoke said.

'They were,' Jack confirmed, 'except for the masks, of course.'

'It's the perfect disguise,' Mr Doyle said.

'I'll get a constable to see if anyone noticed them change,' Greystoke said.

Mr Doyle nodded. 'We may be lucky, but there are two rather more intriguing questions regarding this case.'

'And they are?'

'First of all, why did they steal the Cusco necklace?'

'Surely that's obvious. It's quite valuable.'

'But why take it when there are several other equally precious pieces in the museum that would have been far easier to steal?'

'It *is* rather puzzling,' Greystoke admitted. 'But sometimes people steal pieces for their private collection. The artefact never sees the light of day again.'

'You said you had two questions, Mr Doyle,' Scarlet said.

'Indeed I do,' Mr Doyle said. 'I am wondering exactly where Professor Clarke went.'

Jack was confused about that too. After the robbery, Jack and Scarlet had checked the other museum visitors to see if anyone had been hurt. By the time they came back the professor was hurrying from the room, his bag in tow.

Matthew Pocket appeared from downstairs. They told him about Professor Clarke's rapid departure.

'I met James Clarke a few years ago at a symposium on ancient history,' Pocket said. 'He's a genius, but also rather reclusive.'

'Did you see him today?' Inspector Greystoke asked.

'No. I didn't know he was coming in.' The young man frowned. 'I remember hearing he had a heart condition. I hope he's all right.'

'We should check,' Mr Doyle said to Jack and Scarlet. 'There are twelve hotels within walking distance of the museum. He can't have lugged such an enormous bag far.'

They began the arduous task of trekking from hotel to hotel. The sixth was a modest-looking building near the Thames called The Bainbridge. Mr Doyle inquired about the professor at the front desk.

'He is staying here,' the clerk confirmed. He wore a badge that read *John Mills*. 'But we are not in the habit of handing out the room numbers of our guests. I can have a message sent up, if you like.'

When Mr Doyle explained they were concerned

about the professor's health, Mills sent one of the bellhops to check. He returned a moment later and spoke quietly to the desk clerk. 'There may be something wrong with Professor Clarke,' Mills relayed. 'There's no answer at his door, and it appears to be locked from the inside.'

Jack, Scarlet and Mr Doyle took an elevator to the fifth floor with Mills. At the end of the corridor, Mills pointed to a door, numbered 56. He called Professor Clarke's name, but there was no reply. Mr Doyle tried the handle, then threw himself against the door. Inside they found the old man in a chair facing the window.

'Professor Clarke?' Mr Doyle inquired, rounding the figure and grasping his arm. 'Can you hear me?'

The old man did not make a sound. The detective snapped his fingers a few times, repeating his name.

'What's wrong with him?' Mills asked.

'He seems to be in some sort of trance. He is completely unresponsive.'

Clarke's eyes were open, but they were dilated and unfocused. Occasionally he blinked, but it was a lazy movement as if he were operating in slow motion.

'You'd best send for an ambulance,' Mr Doyle said to Mills. 'This looks quite serious.'

Jack and Scarlet waited for the desk clerk to leave.

'We have another problem,' Scarlet said.

'What is it?' Mr Doyle asked.

'This man isn't Professor Clarke,' Jack said. 'I don't know who he is.'

'What?'

'It's not him.'

'Are you sure?' Mr Doyle asked. 'You did only meet him for a few minutes.'

'Completely,' Scarlet said, examining him. 'He looks similar, but the man we met had a longer face.'

'And his eyes were a different colour,' Jack agreed. 'The man we met had brown eyes. This isn't the same man.'

'How very strange,' the detective said. 'We should search the room.'

Jack looked inside the wardrobe while Scarlet opened drawers. But there wasn't much to find. The professor—if that's who he was—had little in the way of personal effects. Apart from the papers on the desk, he only had a few items of clothing and some toiletries.

'Look at this,' Mr Doyle said, pulling something from the chair. 'It's some kind of thorn.' It was purple and thin as a needle.

'I've never seen anything like it,' Scarlet said.

'It's certainly not native to this country.' The detective examined the professor again. 'There's a small mark under his jaw.' Mr Doyle placed the thorn into a bag. 'Which brings us to another mystery. How did the perpetrator escape this room?'

Good question, Jack thought. *The room was locked from the inside.*

'Could the professor have done this to himself?' he asked.

Mr Doyle tilted his head.

'You already know,' Scarlet said.

'I believe so.'

Ignatius Doyle went to the window and carefully eased it open. A ledge, half a foot wide, ran the length of the building.

'You think someone escaped through the window?' Scarlet said. 'The ledge is very narrow.'

'It could be done,' Jack said, remembering back to his days at the circus. It was all about controlling your balance and remaining calm. 'But it wouldn't be easy. It's a fifty-foot drop.'

'Yet it would seem to be the only possibility.' Mr Doyle leaned out the window. 'And I think I can see where the assailant went. A window leading to the next room is ajar.'

Mills returned. 'I've sent a boy for an ambulance,' he said. 'It should be here in a few minutes.'

'Good,' Ignatius Doyle said. 'Is there anyone staying in this next room?'

'I don't believe so.'

'Please open it for us.'

Mills lent them the key while he guarded the professor. The room next door was identical. Mr Doyle gave a satisfied grunt as he examined the windowsill.

'There's a thread on this window from an orange shirt,' he said, placing the fabric into another small bag. 'I wonder if they found what they were looking for.'

'What do you mean, Mr Doyle?' Jack asked.

'You mentioned Professor Clarke had a large trunk with him earlier, but we have seen no sign of it.'

'The man next door is not him,' Scarlet said firmly.

'Or,' Jack said, 'the man we saw at the museum wasn't the professor.'

'Either way,' Mr Doyle said, 'there is no sign of the bag.'

They returned to the other room. Two ambulance men had just arrived with a stretcher. The professor's condition was unchanged, his eyes wide open, staring into space. Jack found it unnerving.

As they carried the professor away, Mr Doyle turned to the desk clerk. 'Did he leave anything in the hotel safe?'

'One moment.'

They headed downstairs where Mills disappeared into a room behind the front desk. He emerged a minute later, frowning.

'What is it?' Mr Doyle asked.

The clerk looked pained. 'There is something, but hotel regulations do not allow us to disclose that information.'

'Are you sure you can't bend the rules? A man's life may be at stake.'

'It would be my job if I were to tell you,' he said. 'And the reputation of the hotel.'

Mr Doyle nodded. 'I'm sure you won't mind if I ask a friend at Scotland Yard to contact you.'

'Not at all. A request from the police is a completely different matter.'

They bade him goodnight, left the hotel and paused in the early evening air. The sky above London was growing dark. The Metrotower angled up between two buildings, thousands of windows illuminated like small eyes watching over the city. A fog was rolling in. The streets were busy with commuters heading home, steamcars spilling smoke into the air as horse and carts jockeyed for position on the road. The ambulance carrying Professor Clarke—or whoever he was—disappeared around the corner.

Jack shivered, but it wasn't from the cold. He couldn't get the horrible expression on the professor's face from his mind.

'We'll find a tavern to have a meal before we return to Bee Street,' Mr Doyle said. 'I suspect you haven't eaten lunch.'

'We did miss out,' Jack said, suddenly aware of his growling stomach.

'And we'll visit the hospital to check on the professor's condition first thing tomorrow morning,' Mr Doyle said.

But it was not to be.

CHAPTER SIX

'Good heavens!'

Mr Doyle's startled exclamation came halfway through breakfast in the kitchen of 221 Bee Street.

On the small table in the centre sat a cage that contained Bertha, Mr Doyle's cobalt blue tarantula. Jack had lived in mortal terror of the arachnid when he first moved into the apartment, but now he was able to happily live with the spider—as long as she remained in her cage.

'What is it, Mr Doyle?' Jack asked as the detective stared at the newspaper.

'It's the British Museum,' he said. 'It's been robbed.'

Jack caught Scarlet's eye. 'Uh...yes,' he said. 'We

were there when it happened. Don't you remember?'

'Of course I do,' the detective said. 'It's been robbed *again*.'

Within minutes, they were racing in a steamcab through the fog-filled streets towards the museum. Mr Doyle stared out the window, his brow furrowed.

'A second robbery,' Scarlet said. 'Plus the missing… somebody.'

'It's all quite puzzling,' Mr Doyle said. 'I wonder if you've had any thoughts as to why the thieves returned to the museum.'

'Maybe they missed something the first time,' Scarlet suggested.

'Or maybe they left something behind,' Jack said.

'A good idea,' Mr Doyle said.

The scene outside the museum was chaos. Reporters shouted questions. Photographers with cameras on tripods took photos, flash lamps burning. The police struggled to hold back the crowd as spectators pushed forward for a glimpse. Traffic around the museum was at a standstill.

Pushing through the crowd, Mr Doyle entered the main foyer, an enormous room with cathedral ceilings. The museum director, Mr Silas Roylott, was wringing his hands with dismay as he spoke with Inspector Greystoke.

'Ah, Ignatius,' Greystoke said. 'I had a feeling we might see you again.'

'You could not have kept me away with a barge pole.'

'It's a puzzling mystery, to be sure.'

'I don't see how they could have broken in,' Silas Roylott said. 'It's impossible.'

'And yet they have achieved the impossible,' Mr Doyle said.

'Then they must be ghosts,' Mr Roylott said.

Mr Doyle smiled. 'I don't believe in ghosts. Shall we attend the scene? And perhaps you can fill us in on exactly what was stolen.'

'What was stolen was a piece of the Broken Sun.'

Great, Jack thought. *That's cleared everything up.*

The director elaborated as they walked through the museum. 'The Broken Sun is an ancient device, comprised of three pieces, and discovered in the city of Alexandria. It only arrived at the museum this week. The expedition had been privately funded, and Professor Clarke was happy to let us examine his piece. The other two parts are in the hands of private collectors.'

'Professor Clarke?' Mr Doyle said. 'The man who was here yesterday?'

'Yes. I was surprised to learn he had visited the museum, but I was told he was here to deliver some other artefacts.'

'That's what he told us,' Scarlet said.

'And the other collectors?' Mr Doyle asked.

'They are both ancient history experts—Professor Stein of Scotland and Professor Morely of Norway.'

'Why is it called the Broken Sun?' Jack asked.

'Each piece is made from gold, in a similar shape

to a relay baton. They are covered in dials that turn like the wheel of a slot machine. These dials are inscribed with numerous images, but common to each is that of a fractured sun. The pieces are unlike anything ever recovered from the ancient world.'

'It reminds me of a combination lock,' Mr Doyle said.

'They may be,' Roylott admitted. 'But no-one has been able to decode them. We suspect they're designed to slot together into a single shaft, but no-one has even been able to find a way to link them.'

They walked into an elevator and started to descend.

'And how did the thieves enter this time?' Mr Doyle asked.

The elevator came to a stop. They were deep underground. Jack had never seen this part of the building. It looked like a bank vault: a room clad with brick led to a safe room secured by a circular metal door. It was open now and he could see the shelves beyond laden with artefacts. Police were inside looking for breaks in the stonework.

'That's the most baffling part of the mystery,' Roylott said. 'There's no sign of a break-in from outside and the only way to enter the vault is through this door.'

'And no-one entered?'

'There is a guard posted at the end of this corridor. He has worked at the museum for almost thirty years.'

'And so you trust him.'

'Completely. And the door can only be opened by knowing the combination, and only myself and two other directors have that knowledge.'

Ignatius Doyle stood in the centre of the safe room and turned, his eyes focusing on every detail. The floor, ceiling and walls were made of stone. The shelves appeared undisturbed, the artefacts on them carefully labelled.

The detective looked up. 'Where does that lead?' he asked, pointing to a small grille set into the ceiling.

'That's a vertical air vent,' Roylott said, frowning. 'You can't seriously believe that anyone could climb down it? It wouldn't even fit a child.'

'Someone fetch me a chair, please.'

A moment later Mr Doyle peered through the grille with his goggles. 'There appear to be clips attaching it to the vent.' He removed the metal piece and examined the inside. A stone shaft led straight up into darkness. 'Now that's very interesting.'

'What is, Ignatius?' Greystoke asked.

The detective produced a pair of tweezers and removed something from the edge of the grille. He stepped down from the chair, pulled a sheet of paper from his pocket and laid something down on it. 'We've seen this before.'

'Good heavens,' Scarlet said.

'It's a piece of orange thread!' Jack said. 'Just like at the hotel.'

'Indeed.' Mr Doyle turned to Roylott. 'What's above this room?'

'The South American section.'

'Where the first robbery occurred?'

'That's right.'

'Inspector, will you ask one of your constables to assist us?'

Greystoke now called on a tall, gangly colleague to stand on the chair and rap on the inside of the vertical shaft with his truncheon. Mr Doyle asked everyone to follow him upstairs.

The South American section was still closed to the public. The broken display case had been removed, but everything else was unchanged.

Mr Doyle headed to the life-size dioramas. Native people, with tents behind, were grouped around a pretend fire. Mr Doyle paused before the diorama. They all listened hard. A faint rapping sound came from the display; they could hear the police officer from far below. Mr Doyle stepped into the diorama, skirting the mannequins.

'Excuse me, madam,' he said, picking up a mannequin and putting it to one side. 'Ah ha.'

Jack, Scarlet and the others climbed into the display to find Ignatius Doyle examining a vent behind one of the tents. 'This is it,' he said. 'The point of entry.'

Roylott snorted. 'That's ridiculous. That shaft is still too small for a person to fit down.'

'A young child, or an exceptionally small adult, could do it.'

'But how did they enter and leave the museum after hours?'

The detective turned to Jack and Scarlet. 'Do either of you remember anything unusual about the professor?'

'He left very quickly after the robbery,' Jack said.

'He practically *disappeared*,' Scarlet said. 'I was quite surprised, especially considering his age—and the weight of his bag.'

The detective fixed them with a stare. Jack remembered watching the professor leave. He *had* moved very quickly. Prior to the robbery he had struggled to drag his enormous suitcase behind, but afterwards he almost ran away. An unpleasant sensation swam in Jack's stomach as the pieces of the puzzle came together.

No!

Scarlet squealed as the same thought occurred to her.

'Mr Doyle!' she said. 'You don't think—'

'I do,' he said. 'I think the first theft was merely a decoy.'

Inspector Greystoke shook his head. 'I have no idea what you three are talking about. What was a decoy?'

'This is what we believe happened,' Ignatius Doyle said. 'A man posing as Professor James Clarke entered the museum. He was working with the criminals, who arrived shortly after. They started firing their weapons, sending everyone fleeing or diving for cover. The criminals broke into the display case containing the Cusco necklace. With everyone facedown on the floor, the man posing as Professor Clarke carried out his part of the plan.'

'Which was?' Greystoke asked.

'To open his bag,' Jack said, 'and—'

'—release the person inside,' Scarlet concluded. 'They must have been very small. They took refuge in the diorama while the criminals escaped. The police arrived, investigated the scene, and the museum closed shortly after.'

'You mean he purposely left someone here?' Inspector Greystoke said. 'And none of us knew it?'

'Why would anyone search for an intruder?' Mr Doyle asked. 'Everyone thought the crime had already taken place.'

'When the *real* crime was to steal the piece of the Broken Sun after the museum closed,' Jack said.

Mr Roylott looked ill. 'I ordered this section closed off after the robbery. The staff normally run a security sweep of the entire building at closing time. But they skipped this floor.'

'But why go to so much trouble to hide someone in the museum?' Greystoke asked.

'I imagine it is much easier to break into the vault downstairs once you're actually inside,' Mr Doyle said. 'Is that correct, Silas?'

'It is,' Roylott confirmed, dabbing sweat from his brow. 'The building is a fortress at night. Nothing in. Nothing out.'

Inspector Greystoke was now shaking his head in amazement. 'And you're saying the thief stayed here overnight,' he said, 'and walked out scot free?'

'Not at all,' Ignatius Doyle said, grabbing the arm of a figure in the exhibit. 'The thief has been standing here with us the whole time.'

CHAPTER SEVEN

Jack's mouth fell open as the saw the mannequin—or what he had believed to be a mannequin—spring to life. The small man had been so silent, so motionless, that he had blended in perfectly. He was slim and shorter than Jack, with dark skin and cropped black hair. Over his shoulder hung a bag that could only contain one thing—the Broken Sun.

When Mr Doyle went to grab him, the stranger delivered a kick to the detective's abdomen. Mr Doyle slumped to the floor. Inspector Greystoke came next, arms outstretched, but he was knocked into the display, sending mannequins everywhere. The thief sprinted away.

'Stop him!' Mr Roylott yelled.

Jack gave chase, leaping from the diorama and racing across the room. The stranger was lithe and unbelievably fast. An alert police officer tried to grab him, but the thief slapped him to the ground.

He flew out the main doors of the museum. *I can't believe he's so quick*, Jack thought. *He's like an athlete.*

Outside, it had started to rain. Jack followed the thief down a side lane, slipping. The little man also slid and fell, giving Jack a chance to close the gap before the stranger disappeared from sight.

Jack reached the end of the lane, breathing hard. Ahead lay a dilapidated street. A railway line cut across the end. This part of town, like so many in London, was slated for demolition. The rain fell harder, sending the few people on the street racing for cover.

He must have ducked into one of the buildings. But which one?

'Excuse me, sir,' Jack said to a passing man. 'Did you see—'

The man ignored him, hurrying past.

Jack spotted a small boy with red curly hair sitting on a nearby doorstep.

'Did you see a man run down the street?' he asked.

The boy said nothing.

'I've got some candy. Would you like a piece?'

The boy nodded. Jack produced the wrapped piece from his green coat and held it out. Just as the boy reached for it, Jack pulled it away.

'Did you see a man run by here?'

'Yes.'

'Where did he go?'

The boy indicated a building across the road. Jack handed him the sweet and ran to the house. The house was sandwiched between brick terraces, most of them burnt out, and its front windows were boarded up, the door secured with a bolt and padlock, the bottom panel broken.

Jack peered through the gap to see a pair of legs scuttling up a flight of rickety stairs. He squeezed through the door. Mould covered the carpet in large charcoal patches and paint peeled from the walls in great strips like flayed skin. The place smelt of mildew, the *plop plop* of dripping water echoing along the hall.

Jack's heart pounded, his face hot and flushed. It wasn't just from the pursuit. He was afraid. The man knew he was being followed. And he was dangerous. Jack paused, wondering if there might be a better method than confrontation.

'My name is Jack Mason,' he called up the stairwell. 'All I want is to get the artefact back to the museum.'

He strained to hear, but the rain was falling so hard the man could have been dancing a jig for all he knew.

'I'm not interested in taking you to the police. Just give me the piece of the Broken Sun and you can go free.'

More silence.

Jack began up the stairs. The first floor landing opened out onto three doors. Two were open to rooms lined with more peeling wallpaper, and rotting

63

floorboards. A pile of beer bottles lay in one. The other contained a broken kerosene lamp. Water poured through holes in the ceiling.

I guess that only leaves number three.

Slowly easing it open, Jack saw another empty room, but this time the window was open. As he stepped forward, someone grabbed him from behind.

Jack bit back a scream and jumped half a foot into the air.

'Scarlet!' he hissed. 'What are you doing here?'

'Taking a walk in the park! What do you think I'm doing?' She looked like she'd taken a dip in the Thames. 'Where's the thief?'

'I'm not sure,' Jack said. 'Wait here.'

He crossed the room. With every step the floor shuddered. The building was ready for demolition. Too much weight on these floorboards might bring the whole place down.

Jack reached the window. The little man could not have escaped through it. There was no ledge to gain a foothold. Carefully tiptoeing back, Jack said, 'This isn't safe. You shouldn't be here.'

'You're right,' Scarlet said. 'I'll go home and take up knitting.'

'All right, but be careful.'

'I can look after myself.'

The next floor was identical, except the pressed-tin ceilings of the rooms had been removed, exposing the joists and rafters. The sound of the rain hitting the slate roof was even louder.

The rooms were also empty. Shooting Scarlet a glance, Jack cautiously eased open the final door. Inside the window was wide open, rain driven in by a howling wind.

He must have escaped onto the roof.

Scarlet pushed past. Jack told her to stop, but she didn't hear him. She was halfway across when the floor gave a violent shudder. It groaned, shook and began to collapse.

'No!' Jack yelled.

He threw himself at Scarlet, dragging her towards the window. They both reached for the sill just as the floor disappeared.

It slammed into the floor below. And the floor below it. The sound was like an avalanche and dust choked the air. The racket subsided, replaced by the sound of the pouring rain. Jack pulled himself up, dragging Scarlet after him. They balanced on the sill. The front of the building still stood, but the interior had been reduced to rubble.

'Oh dear,' Scarlet said, looking at the debris. 'What a nuisance.'

'If facing certain death can be called a nuisance, then I suppose it is.'

'Don't be silly.' She punched him in the shoulder. 'Still, thanks for saving my life.'

'That's all right. You can help rearrange my stamp collection later.'

Jack looked across the adjoining roofs. The man was long gone, but the demolition had brought people into the street. Jack called down, 'Would you mind getting the police? And the fire brigade?'

An hour later Jack and Scarlet were back at the British Museum. Mr Doyle admonished them for risking their lives.

'Did you not hear me calling after you?' he growled. 'You must stop taking these terrible risks. We know very little about these people. You might have been killed.'

Jack and Scarlet promised to be more careful.

'Where do we go from here?' Scarlet asked.

'Home. I have sent for some information and I believe it will be there when we arrive.'

'Information?'

'You'll see.'

They hailed a steamcab and headed back to Bee Street. After Jack and Scarlet had changed, they had a lunch of cucumber sandwiches prepared by Gloria in the sitting room. A message arrived and Mr Doyle read it.

'We've had some success,' Mr Doyle said. 'I have the addresses of the other two men who first discovered the Broken Sun.'

He picked up a parcel that had also been delivered, removed a book and leafed through it.

'What is it, Mr Doyle?' Scarlet asked.

'This is what Professor Clarke had hidden in the safe at the hotel. Scotland Yard were kind enough to forward it on.'

'That might be what the thief was looking for,' Jack said. 'Is it helpful?'

'Hmm.' The detective raised an eyebrow. 'You tell me.'

Jack started reading. Scarlet peered over his shoulder and stifled a laugh.

'Oh dear,' she said. 'That's most unexpected.'

'Asparagus soup,' Jack read. 'Shortbread, lasagne, tomatoes stuffed with mushroom and garlic risotto.' He looked up. 'It's a cookbook.'

'Unfortunately, yes,' Mr Doyle said. 'It seems the professor is rather a keen chef. At least we still have the other men from the expedition.'

'Do you think their lives are in danger?' Scarlet asked.

'Undoubtedly. Whoever stole the Broken Sun from the museum will be after the other pieces. The closest is in Scotland, held by Professor Richard Stein. We will leave shortly.'

Gloria appeared. 'She's ready and waiting,' she said.

'*She*?' Jack said.

Mr Doyle smiled. 'Who do you think?'

He led them to the far end of the building, which opened out onto a balcony. A set of stairs took them to the roof where they found an airship moored—the *Lion's Mane*.

The vessel had been badly damaged after they had pursued one of the world's most deadly assassins, a man known as the Chameleon.

The *Lion's Mane* was thirty-feet long with a gondola made from brass and timber. Steam propelled the airship from two tubes beneath the gondola, and beneath these were four other pipes that discharged smoke from the engine and a pair of skids for landing.

'She looks wonderful, Mr Doyle,' Scarlet breathed.

'As good as new,' Jack echoed.

'*Better*,' said the detective. 'I've made some improvements. There is now a refrigerator on board.'

'A refrigerator?' Jack said. 'That's amazing.'

Mr Doyle nodded. 'Refrigeration is one of the wonders of the modern age,' he said.

'Will you be using it to preserve forensic samples?' Scarlet asked.

The detective looked surprised. 'What a wonderful idea,' he said. 'I just thought it would store cheese.'

The engine had already been brought to the boil.

'I need both of you to pack bags,' the detective said. 'We will be away for a few days. And Jack, can you see to Bertha?'

Jack headed to his room, a neat and tidy chamber with an en-suite bathroom. Back at the orphanage, he had shared a room of this size with a dozen other boys. A duck egg sat in the middle of his bed; Mr Doyle was always leaving items in his room to test his powers of observation.

Jack had fallen into the habit of keeping a small bag packed with a change of clothing, which he grabbed before retrieving Bertha from the kitchen. He walked through to reception where Gloria was typing.

'We're going to be away for a few days,' he told her. 'Will you be able to—'

'—look after the girl?' Gloria said, smiling. 'Of course.' She placed the cage on her desk. 'Looks like it's you and me, my dear.'

A few minutes later Jack, Scarlet and Mr Doyle were high above the streets of London, heading north in a line of airships. Jack loved watching the passing scenery. The new Houses of Parliament were on the Thames, several hundred feet east of Westminster. One hundred stories high, they were shaped like two domed drums stuck together. The top of each was decorated with a huge brass lion.

Soon the city was behind them and they were crossing farms and green hills. Jack watched fields filled with pumpkins the size of steamcars and eight-legged horses, inventions courtesy of the Darwinist League. He pointed them out to Scarlet.

'We live in an incredible era,' she said. 'But I suppose there are some things that will never be improved upon.'

'Like what?'

'Steam, for example,' she said, her red hair glowing in the afternoon sunlight.

Jack's eyes settled on her. She really *was* the most beautiful girl he had ever seen.

'You're right,' he said dreamily. 'You can't beat it.'

CHAPTER EIGHT

'Welcome to Scotland,' Mr Doyle said.

While much of Britain was industrialised, great swathes of it still remained wild and remote. Scotland was like this, where most of its people still lived as they had for centuries. Some grew crops on small landholdings—oats, wheat and rye—tilling the ground with wooden ploughs dragged by draft horses. Other farms kept sheep and goats. Many towns were small, with no more than half-a-dozen homes, a pub and general store.

Jack had toured Scotland a few times with his parents in the circus. He felt a pang of sadness, touching the compass and picture in his pocket. They had been hard times, but some of the happiest in his life.

'Where are we headed?' Scarlet asked as Mr Doyle angled the *Lion's Mane* towards the coast.

'To a small town called Wick. Professor Stein was one of the experts to discover the Broken Sun. Originally from the United States, he now resides in a castle known as Castle Wick.'

'Castle Wick in the town of Wick,' Jack said.

Mr Doyle winked at them. 'Let's hope he's not wick-ed.'

Jack and Scarlet groaned.

'It was a ruin,' Mr Doyle went on, 'until it was restored several years ago. Hopefully it will still have the same fortifications.'

They travelled on in silence. Mr Doyle followed the shoreline until they were almost at the most north-eastern point of the mainland. Beyond here Jack could see only the specks of land that made up the Orkney Islands.

Mr Doyle gave a grunt of satisfaction and brought the airship down in a meadow. Castle Wick was a large square structure with battlements, perched perilously close to a cliff face overlooking the sea. To Jack's eyes the building looked authentic; whoever had done the restoration had done a fine job of it.

Scarlet pointed to one of the windows. 'I just saw a curtain move.'

'They probably don't get many visitors in this part of the country,' Mr Doyle said. 'I hope the professor is gracious.'

The entrance was an oak door set into the stonework.

It swung open as they approached and a gaunt man, reminiscent of a praying mantis, appeared. 'State your business!' he snapped, with the trace of an American accent. 'My time is precious!'

'Are you Professor Stein?'

'I am.'

'We believe you may be in great danger.'

'Danger? What kind of danger?'

'A piece of the Broken Sun has been stolen from the British Museum.'

'That's garbage! Impossible!'

Jack shot Scarlet a look.

And we came here to help this man?

'I'm afraid it is the case,' Mr Doyle said.

The professor's eyes narrowed. 'I see. And you think someone may be coming here to steal my piece of the map? Castle Wick is impregnable. Nothing can breach its defences.'

'Yet you have been worried,' Mr Doyle said.

Stein folded his arms. 'What gives you that idea?'

'You were cleaning your gun this morning.'

The professor blinked. 'How the hell—'

'It is simplicity itself. There is a distinctive mark on your left hand that results from the cleaning of a revolver. In addition, I can smell the oil used on such a weapon.'

For the first time, Richard Stein's confidence was shaken. His eyes searched the open fields behind them. 'I am simply being cautious,' he said. 'The Broken Sun is a priceless artefact.'

'Have you checked it today?'

'There is no need.'

'I suggest you do so.'

'The impudence—' Stein almost bounced up and down with anger. Somehow he regained control of himself. 'Wait here!'

The door slammed.

'What a lovely man,' Mr Doyle said. 'We must invite him for Christmas.'

'What will we do now?' Jack asked.

Mr Doyle sighed. 'Helping a man who claims to not need assistance is rather problematic. It would seem—' But he did not finish. A shot rang out. 'What the devil!'

There was a cry, and another shot from inside. Mr Doyle pushed against the door; the professor had not bolted it. They rushed through a cloakroom into a foyer decorated with armour and family crests. Up a winding staircase, they found Professor Stein on the floor in the hallway, his face white with terror.

He pointed into a room with a shaking hand. 'There!' he cried. 'There!'

Jack caught a glimpse of a figure disappearing through the window—the black-haired man from the museum. Jack tore to the window, only to see the man scuttling down the wall like a spider.

'My goodness!' Scarlet said.

Jack was amazed. He had never seen anyone climb with such ease and he was holding a piece of the

Broken Sun! The gold baton, with its myriad of strange symbols, glittered in the sunlight.

The professor lurched into the room. 'You must retrieve the artefact!' he shouted. 'It's priceless!'

They raced out of the castle. The thief was sprinting across a field towards a hill. Jack started after him, but Mr Doyle grabbed his arm and pointed back to the *Lion's Mane*.

'He must have transportation,' Mr Doyle said. 'If he does, we'll never catch him on foot.'

Mr Doyle was right. No sooner had they risen above the field did they see another small airship taking off.

But Mr Doyle had them over the water in seconds. The thief's airship was faster than the *Lion's Mane*. He headed to a tiny island and rapidly descended to the beach. Mr Doyle landed just as the man disappeared inland on foot.

'Best have Clarabelle ready,' the detective said, drawing his gun as they left the airship. 'Stay behind me.'

They made their way over a sandy knoll. The island was a wild, windswept place, covered in jagged hills and crevices. Flurries of sand danced over rocky dunes. Birds soared overhead, singing mournful songs. They followed a trail of footsteps until Mr Doyle grunted and drew to a halt.

'There's something wrong here,' he said, pointing at the prints. 'They are deeper at the heel than the toe.'

'Why is that strange?' Jack asked.

'If he is running—which we can assume he is—his toes should be sinking into the ground first. Unless...' The detective snapped his fingers. 'What a fool I am! He has doubled back behind us.'

They raced back the way they had come. Another set of prints had already disturbed their own. Just as they reached the shore, they glimpsed the *Lion's Mane* taking off towards the coast.

'That scoundrel!' Mr Doyle snapped. 'He's stolen our ship!'

The thief's vessel lay moored on the beach, the name on the bow identifying it as the *Pimpernel*. They climbed aboard, only to find that the control panel had been smashed beyond repair.

Jack watched the *Lion's Mane* disappear into the clouds.

'He's getting away,' Mr Doyle said, 'and we're stuck on this island with no way to return.'

CHAPTER NINE

It was cold and dark on the island. The *Pimpernel* had blankets, but no pillows or food supplies. Mr Doyle started a fire while the team turned to their emergency supplies for sustenance.

'Beef jerky,' Jack said, biting down on the hard meat. 'There's nothing quite like it.'

'There is, actually,' Mr Doyle said, warming his hands. 'I once ate my belt. It had a similar taste.'

'You ate—' Scarlet stopped. 'Mr Doyle, did you say you once ate your *belt*?'

'I did. I was stranded in the Carpathian Mountains without food and water. It was either eat my clothing or die of starvation.'

'How horrible.'

'It tasted far better than my boots,' Mr Doyle said, shuddering. 'I still have nightmares about those boots.'

The wind came up and they huddled around the fire. Jack's eyes settled on Scarlet. She was an incredible girl. There was never a word of complaint from her. It seemed her spirit could not be quashed.

And she was so pretty! Even now her tangled hair, cast about by the breeze, perfectly framed her pixie face. And her eyes were as green as a deep forest. Her lips—

'What's wrong?' Scarlet demanded, staring at him.

'Huh?'

'You're grinning at me oddly. Is there something in my hair?'

'No!' Jack blushed. 'I was just thinking.'

'Well don't! It doesn't suit you!'

The temperature continued to drop. It may have been spring, but the strong onshore wind was icy. They kept an eye on the water, but no ships came into sight. The discussion returned to the case. Jack was enthusiastic that they had possession of the thief's vessel until Mr Doyle pointed out it was stolen.

'There are papers on board indicating the *Pimpernel* belongs to a Lady Jefferson of Sussex. She appears to own two dachshunds named Zali and Koko,' he said. 'I have taken note of the airship's registration number, but I doubt it will lead to anything.'

Early the next morning, Mr Doyle managed to hail a passing fishing boat that took them back to the mainland. They ate a hearty meal in town before heading to Professor Stein's castle. He was able to add little to what he had already told them: the robbery was still a mystery to him—as was the theft from the British Museum.

'Professor Stein is lying,' Mr Doyle said as they travelled on a train back to London. 'He knows more than he's letting on. We did learn one thing that may help us. The professor made a small slip about the artefact when we met him.'

Jack thought hard. 'He said the Broken Sun was part of a map.'

'Good boy.'

'It's hard to believe that odd contraption could be part of a map,' Scarlet mused.

'There have been many strange maps throughout history,' Mr Doyle said. 'One of the most unusual was a medieval German map of the world made by Gervase of Ebstorf. Measuring twelve feet wide, it was constructed from the skin of thirty goats.'

They arrived back at Bee Street a few hours later. Gloria threw together an impromptu lunch of sausages and potatoes, and Jack and Scarlet ate in the sitting room while Mr Doyle leafed through his mail. Jack turned to see a goldfish bowl filled with glass eyes. He was sure it hadn't been there before.

Gloria stuck her head in. 'I have good news,' she said. 'The *Lion's Mane* has been found abandoned in Edmonton.'

'Is she damaged?' Mr Doyle asked.

Gloria confirmed the vessel was in excellent condition and already on route to them. The reception bell rang and she went to answer it, returning with a business card.

'There's a gentleman to see you,' she said. 'Tobias Bradstreet.'

'The mining tycoon?' Mr Doyle frowned. 'Did he state his business?'

'Something about being able to help you with your investigation.'

Scarlet bit her lip. 'How would he know what we're investigating?'

'That is a mystery,' Mr Doyle said. 'Show him in, Gloria.'

The man who stepped through the door was tall and thin with steel grey hair and broad shoulders. He carried a grave air about him, but he still smiled as he shook hands and took a seat.

'I'll get straight to the point,' Bradstreet said. 'I know you're involved in the investigation of some stolen artefacts. I also have an interest in retrieving those same pieces.'

'I am curious to know how you found out about our investigation,' Mr Doyle said.

'Let's just say I have eyes and ears everywhere. I would like to engage your services.'

'I am already employed by the British Museum. Obviously any information about the Broken Sun would be helpful.' Mr Doyle paused. 'I assume you're one of the investors who backed the original expedition.'

'I am. I've long had an interest in archaeology.'

'What is so important about the Broken Sun?'

'Let me ask you a question,' Bradstreet said. 'What do you know about Atlantis?'

'Atlantis?' Mr Doyle frowned. 'It's a mythical city, first mentioned in the writings of Plato around 360 BC. Supposedly it was destroyed by a disaster some 10,000 years ago.'

'What if I told you it wasn't a myth?'

'Surely you don't believe that?'

'I do.'

'Why?'

Bradstreet shook his head. 'Let's just say I've come across some evidence that confirms it was as real as London is today.'

'I find that hard to believe,' Mr Doyle said. 'Even ancient scholars thought it imaginary. It has only been in recent times that people have believed it really existed.'

'It did exist and I intend to find it.'

Scarlet ran her hands through her hair. 'So the pieces of the Broken Sun are some kind of map? A map that leads to Atlantis?'

Bradstreet nodded. 'The evidence indicates Atlantis was an island in the Atlantic Ocean located to the west of Gibraltar. The cataclysm that destroyed it did so in a day and a night. It has been long rumoured that the Atlanteans were decimated by their own technology.' He clenched his fists. 'But I believe the map leads to something far more valuable.'

'More valuable than Atlantis?' Jack asked.

'Indeed. I believe it points to the location of *New* Atlantis.'

'New Atlantis?' Mr Doyle said. 'You think the Atlanteans survived the disaster?'

'Of course they did!' Bradstreet stood and began to pace the room. 'They were an advanced race. Years ahead of anyone else. They could not be destroyed in one fell swoop! They escaped the disaster and rebuilt their empire. The question is, *where*?'

'It's a very entertaining story,' Mr Doyle said. 'However, I'm not a treasure hunter, I'm a detective. I doubt I can be of assistance to you.'

'We are on the same path,' Bradstreet urged. 'Why not work together to solve one of history's greatest mysteries?'

'I'm *not* a treasure hunter.'

Tobias Bradstreet pursed his lips. 'I can double what the British Museum is paying you. Triple it.'

'I'm sorry.'

Bradstreet sighed. 'That is a shame. With my money and resources, you could have been part of the most incredible investigation of your life. I would have thought more of the famous Ignatius Doyle.'

Mr Doyle smiled. 'I'm sorry I don't live up to my reputation.'

The men shook hands and Tobias Bradstreet departed.

'Atlantis!' Jack said. 'I thought it was only a legend!'

'It *is* only a legend,' Mr Doyle said.

'Although,' Scarlet said, 'there is often a foundation for legends. The story of Dracula was based on a medieval tyrant named Vlad the Impaler. And sailors are thought to have mistaken dugongs on rocky shorelines for mermaids.'

'It's possible such a city once existed, but whatever truth surrounds it has been long lost to history.'

'What will we do now?' Jack asked.

'There is still a remaining piece of the Broken Sun to consider. It resides with Professor Howard Morely, a resident of Norway. I have already sent him a message that he may be in danger. Tomorrow we'll leave to visit him to see if he can shed any light on the matter.'

Jack was too excited to sleep. Climbing into bed, his mind was still buzzing.

Atlantis, he thought. *Was it really possible…?*

The next thing he knew was that someone was knocking at his door. He blearily raised his head to see Mr Doyle.

'Adventure calls.'

'Was I asleep?' Jack asked.

'For about three hours.'

'It felt like three minutes.'

'You can grab more sleep on the way. The *Lion's Mane* has been returned and appears to be in perfect order.'

Jack and Scarlet joined Mr Doyle on the roof.

It was a pleasure to see the airship back in her usual position.

Mr Doyle sighed. 'I'm so glad you're here.'

'Thank you, Mr Doyle,' Scarlet said.

'Oh.' The detective looked embarrassed. 'I was actually talking to the ship.' He disengaged the tie ropes and brought the engine to full power. 'Next stop,' he said, 'Norway.'

CHAPTER TEN

It took a full day and a night to cross the North Sea. The lightening sky was wild with scudding clouds, and the wind howled as the thrumming engines pushed the *Lion's Mane* onwards.

Mr Doyle was an excellent pilot, but strong headwinds kept buffeting the vessel about like a cork in a stream, until they finally crossed into Norwegian airspace.

'Did you know that Norway has one of the most rugged coastlines in the world?'

Jack and Scarlet clung to a rail as the *Lion's Mane* tilted wildly, but Mr Doyle seemed completely at ease.

'No, I didn't,' Jack said. 'We're not about to crash into it, are we?'

'Not at all,' the detective laughed heartily. 'What can you tell me about Norway?'

The ship seesawed in the other direction.

'Uh…a lot of Norwegians live there.'

'I must have a word to Miss Bloxley about your geography,' Mr Doyle grumbled.

Scarlet spoke up. 'Norway is known as the Land of the Midnight Sun,' she said. 'For some months of the year, the sun never completely descends below the horizon.'

'Imagine that,' Jack said.

The ship rocked.

Mr Doyle pushed a button on the console. 'Oh dear,' he said. 'That's very unfortunate.'

'What is?' Jack's voice had gone up a key. 'Is something broken?'

'I'm afraid so. I certainly didn't prepare for this.'

Jack tried to remember the evacuation procedures for the ship. He was supposed to put on an inflatable lifejacket. Did he blow it up now? Or when he was in the water? And was it every man for himself? But he couldn't leave Scarlet behind! Or Mr Doyle, for that matter…

'The refrigerator has lost power,' the detective said. 'My cheese will be off.'

'*Your cheese*…?' Scarlet gaped.

'I know,' Mr Doyle said. 'I'm disappointed too.'

Jack and Scarlet held on to the console as the airship tilted in the other direction.

'I think Miss Bloxley might have mentioned Norway.' Jack had learnt more about geography, history, literature and languages in the last few months than in his whole life. 'But it must have slipped my mind.'

'The country of Norway has slipped your mind? The Norwegians would be less than pleased to hear that!' Mr Doyle said as the *Lion's Mane* seesawed again. 'Exhilarating, isn't it?'

'Quite!' Scarlet replied, crashing into Jack.

'Goodness,' Jack grunted.

'Here's an interesting fact for you,' Mr Doyle said. 'Norway is growing larger.'

Jack peeped through the window at the ground, hoping its growth was not simply because they were about to crash into it.

'The entire country was covered in an enormous sheet of ice during the last ice age,' Mr Doyle explained. 'It is now, if you like, "bouncing back" from the weight of that sheet because of a process known as isostatic rebound.'

The ship was hit by a gust that almost knocked Jack and Scarlet off their feet.

Bazookas. Jack knew his mentor was never without a book, even wandering about the rooms at Bee Street with a volume in hand—and they were often on the most scholarly subjects. Last week Mr Doyle had been on the back landing reading something entitled *The Glorious History of Corsets and Their Tight Reign on British Society.*

The wild winds eased and the detective steered the *Lion's Mane* inland. Jack and Scarlet watched the landscape with interest. Mountains and ice and forests and inland bodies of water stretched in all directions. Mr Doyle explained that the country had many towns and cities, but the population was sparsely scattered through the countryside.

He finally landed in a forested valley, swathed in snow. Jack tethered the *Lion's Mane* as Mr Doyle shut off the engine.

The detective stepped from the vessel, clapping his hands together. 'We must come here later in the year,' he said. 'Norway enjoys quite warm temperatures during summer.'

Jack found it hard to believe. 'You mean it has more than ice and snow?'

'It's a lovely place to visit. Ask any Norwegian.'

Jack felt his cheeks turn rosy as they donned overcoats. It was *freezing*. After consulting a map, Mr Doyle found a trail and they began a long march down the hillside. Snow-covered pines surrounded them. The landscape lay strangely quiet in the morning twilight, as if a blanket smothered everything.

It started snowing. Light flurries danced across the landscape as they followed a wide, rocky path. The trail looked like it had been worn down by years of travel. Mr Doyle pointed to a house on the far side of the valley, a small wooden hut, painted red, nestled among the trees.

'I believe that is Professor Morely's residence,' he

said. 'We should reach it within the hour.'

'I hope his reception is a little warmer than Professor Stein's,' Scarlet said.

'Let's hope he doesn't give us the cold shoulder,' Mr Doyle said, winking.

'You notice, of course,' Scarlet mused as they trooped on, 'that these professors are all men?'

'You'll get no argument from me, my dear,' Mr Doyle said. 'Education should be open to all.'

'And yet it is not. Such inequality is unfair.'

Jack had not thought much about women's rights before he met Scarlet, but his mind had been slowly opened to the inequalities between the sexes. There were protests taking place with increasing regularity in England. Many women, including Emmeline Pankhurst, were fighting so that women could have the same rights as men: the right to vote, the right to education and the right to equal employment.

'One day it will change,' Jack said. 'I'm sure.'

'It can't be soon enough for me,' Scarlet said.

'Although I hope it will be peaceful change,' Mr Doyle murmured.

'I assume you're referring to the Valkyrie Circle?' Scarlet asked. It was a terrorist organisation responsible for several bombings around London over the past year. 'I hope so too.'

Two hours later they passed through a low stone wall ringing the property, continuing up a path to the front door.

Mr Doyle motioned them to stop. 'This door is ajar,' he said. 'We may be too late.'

He pulled out his gun as they entered. A small antechamber lined with jackets and hats opened out onto a living room with a fire burning in the corner. It was probably cosy under normal circumstances, but now it felt sinister. Statues and African masks filled the interior while the walls were plastered with sketches of ancient cities and plans for old buildings. Mr Doyle placed a finger over his lips.

Quiet.

He pointed to a narrow staircase. Tiptoeing to the first floor, they heard a sound like drawers being opened. A dissatisfied grunt came from within.

Mr Doyle pushed the door wide. 'It's time we had a little talk.'

The person on the other side of the desk was the same small, black-haired man Jack had previously encountered. Now he wore a white coat and shoes. The contents of filing cabinets and the bookcase had been emptied all over the floor. The man glanced at them casually, his eyes narrowing.

'We have nothing to discuss.' The man might have been small, but he had a surprisingly deep voice. 'The Broken Sun does not belong to you.'

'Nor does it belong to you,' Mr Doyle said, waving the gun. 'Do not take another step.'

'Are you afraid?' the man asked mildly. 'Surely you do not fear one so tiny?'

A sound came from a closed wardrobe. It diverted Mr Doyle for the briefest of moments—enough for the stranger to act. He swung about in a roundhouse kick and knocked Clarabelle away, before delivering a series of lightning-fast blows at Mr Doyle's chest.

The detective fended them off and delivered a right cross to the man's jaw. He staggered from the blow. At first it seemed he was about to collapse, but instead he rolled, catapulting himself between Mr Doyle's legs and into Jack's stomach, driving him against the wall.

Scarlet approached, fist raised, but he swept a leg under her feet and she crashed to the floor. The man kept moving, racing down the hall. Jack, sucking air into his lungs, gave chase.

CHAPTER ELEVEN

The man raced along the path. It was snowing harder now; his white outfit allowed him to blend with the landscape as he disappeared between two pine trees.

Jack's eyes searched the landscape. Then a shadow moved across the snow. Jack leapt backwards as the man slammed into the ground. He had been up one of the trees!

Jack was just in time to deflect a punch, but the man followed up with another thump to the side of his head that knocked him backwards into the snow.

Shaking off the blow, Jack raced after him. The man glanced back and now Jack saw a look of frustration cross his face.

You think you're sick of running? Jack thought savagely. *I'm sick of chasing you.*

Something stirred in Jack's gut, a sense of grim determination. The thief had bested him twice. Once, at the museum, and again on the island. They had already lost two pieces of the Broken Sun. Jack was not prepared to lose the third.

The man dashed up the hill and took the left fork in the path. He was moving more slowly now. Possibly his airship was close by.

Jack put on more speed. His head was throbbing with the exertion and the sharp sting of the cold mountain air. The ground grew steeper, but now he was less than fifty feet away.

Forty feet. Thirty…

The thief disappeared over a rise. A few seconds later, an airship leapt to full power just as Jack reached the gondola. He jumped, but his fingers missed the bottom of the gondola by inches.

Damn!

The airship climbed rapidly towards a bank of low-lying cloud. Jack watched in despair, breathing so hard he was shaking. He had come *so close*.

Snow drifted down from the steel-grey sky, stinging his eyes as the airship entered more cloud.

Bang! Bang!

The shots lacked aim—most likely they were fired as a warning. Jack zigzagged down the hill to some trees.

'Damn,' he said again. 'Damn. Damn. Damn.'

He leaned against a trunk, filled with a despair so powerful he wanted to weep. Three times the thief had been within his grasp and three times he had escaped.

Jack shivered. The cold was starting to take hold again, despite the sweat dripping into his eyes.

His vision blurred. It looked like the ground was moving. Jack stared hard. The ground *was* moving. Further up the hill, it was shuddering as if a ton of popcorn had been dumped onto a dance floor. The blanket of snow covering the hill was sliding, the mountain groaning as if in pain.

'Bazookas,' Jack said. 'It's an avalanche!'

He started down the hill as the roar grew louder, balls of loose snow tumbling past him. Jack ran as fast as he could, but in his panic he had lost the path and now his legs sunk into deeper snow.

Where's the path? he thought. *I'm dead if I don't find it.*

He spotted it, a trail of stone to his left, but it was too late: the entire side of the hill was racing after him like an out-of-control train.

Jack's mind went blank.

He had to think. *Think!*

He had read something about avalanches, that book about mountain climbing in the library back at Bee Street. There was a strange, obscure detail that had fascinated him. What was it? He had to remember or *he was going to die.*

93

Backstroke.

The single word came to him like an explosion. He had to swim in the direction of the avalanche, but freestyle would only cause him to bury himself deeper into the snow. So he had to be counterintuitive: turn his back on the monster racing towards him and *backstroke* over it.

Jack threw himself backwards as the snow swept under his legs, backstroking into the current. The white mass roared past him. Onto him. Still, he forced himself to swim into the behemoth as it swept over him, pouring over his face and body, growing thicker and heavier.

He was surrounded by a choking white haze. It was all around him. Up. Down. Pressing against him from every direction, crushing him like a cold blanket. Now the roar of the avalanche had passed and a terrible silence replaced it.

With an almighty effort, Jack pulled one arm towards his face and created an air pocket. Dragging his other arm free, he burrowed out a space about a foot wide. He had to get out of here, but he wasn't sure which way was up and which way was down.

He didn't want to start digging in the wrong direction because he might get himself deeper into the snow. He was already freezing. And exhausted. He would be dead within minutes. He had to tunnel towards the surface, but where was that?

He spat.

Much to his relief, the drool fell immediately across his chin.

Good old gravity, he thought. *And good old Miss Bloxley.*

Without her, and that blasted book she had lent him, he would have had no chance at all. But he wasn't out of danger yet. He pulled his legs towards him, rolled about and pushed down. Hard. He moved, not far, but far enough. He thrust downwards again. And again.

The air around him was running out. He had to stay calm. Panicking would only use up his precious oxygen, but his heart was racing like a roller-coaster. Jack took three deep breaths and pushed downwards again. It was impossible to tell how much snow was between him and the surface. It could be inches. Or feet.

His fingers and face were now completely numb. If he didn't find the surface soon—

His left elbow met air.

Yes!

He pulled himself up and his head emerged. He saw grey sky and mountains. He breathed in. Air. *Glorious air!*

'Jack!' Scarlet's voice came from nowhere.

Then Mr Doyle was dragging at him. 'Hold on, my boy,' he said. 'We'll have you out in a jiffy.'

Jack tried to mumble that he was fine, but he couldn't form words. His lips would not work. They dragged him free and wrapped themselves around him to warm his body. There were tears in Mr Doyle's eyes.

'You're safe,' he said. 'You're safe, you're safe…'

An hour later they were sitting around Professor Howard Morely's fireplace, drinking tea. Returning to the house, they had found the professor bound and gagged in one of his closets and immediately went to his aid.

'I owe you my life,' he said. 'I'm not sure how I will ever repay you.'

The professor was a small, round man, balding with a grey beard. He clenched his cup of tea with fingers too pudgy to fit through the handle.

'No repayment is necessary,' Mr Doyle said. 'However, we would appreciate some information.'

'It's the least I can do.'

'We have been told that some people believe the Broken Sun is actually a map that points to New Atlantis. Is there any truth in this?'

The professor clenched his jaw. 'That was Clarke and Stein's belief. I didn't share in their pursuit of the mythical city. My interest was in the craftsmanship of the Broken Sun. Nothing like it has ever been found in the ancient world—and I doubt ever will be again.'

'But Clarke and Stein *were* trying to find New Atlantis?'

Professor Morely nodded.

'May I ask, then,' Scarlet said, 'why weren't the pieces of the Broken Sun kept together?'

'It was simply a matter of finance,' the professor explained. 'The expedition was funded by a number of sources, including the British Museum. The contract stated that any findings would be shared between the participants.

'James Clarke and Richard Stein have spent years chasing Atlantis. Some might even call it an obsession. Ancient mysteries are like that sometimes. Intelligent people are swayed from the world of academia and science, turning instead to treasure hunts and riddles.'

Jack asked, 'So what does the Broken Sun do?'

Morely shrugged. 'I have no idea. It is a highly complex device. I assume the three batons lock together to form a single shaft, but we could never get them to join.' He took a sip of tea. 'But that's hardly surprising given the number of combinations.'

'What do you mean?'

Professor Morely smiled sadly. 'Have you worked out how many possible sequences there are?' he asked. 'Two of the Broken Sun pieces have ten dials. The third has seven. It would take a hundred years to try every single combination.'

Mr Doyle frowned. 'So even if the pieces were brought back together…'

'Knowing the correct sequence would take forever.' Morely paused. 'Unless there is a clue to be found in the ancient legends.'

'Who would know such a thing?'

'I do know of someone who is an expert in the field.'

'Who is it?'

'A woman. She is the daughter of famed Egyptian archaeologist, Nathanial Carfax.'

Mr Doyle started, almost dropping his tea. 'Phoebe Carfax?'

'You know her?'

'From my youth,' Mr Doyle said, his face reddening. 'I have not seen her for many years.'

'She resides on the Greek island of Kasos. It is to her that I sent my piece of the Broken Sun.'

Scarlet, Jack and Mr Doyle stared at the professor.

'I thought you knew,' Morely said, surprised. 'After I received your warning message, I sent the piece away. I thought it would be safer with Miss Carfax. I thought she might have a better chance of cracking the puzzle.'

'I hope you won't mind if we contact her.'

'I believe you should.' Professor Morely gave him Phoebe Carfax's address. 'She must be warned her life may be in danger.'

Mr Doyle, Jack and Scarlet made their way back over the snow-covered hills to the *Lion's Mane*. Night was falling, so Mr Doyle decided to delay their departure until the next morning. Jack prepared a meal in the galley while Scarlet set the table. It was a simple dinner—rehydrated vegetables and dried chicken—but it tasted like heaven after the day's exertions.

'So Miss Carfax is an old friend,' Scarlet said innocently, slicing into a piece of meat.

'From your younger days,' Jack added.

Mr Doyle blushed. 'You are both clearly acquiring keen powers of observation.' He smiled. 'We were... acquaintances. I met her at Oxford University.'

'I thought women weren't allowed at universities?' Scarlet said.

'They are not. She was not a student, but her father was in charge of the Ancient History department. She learnt both from him and the university library. Even then Phoebe's knowledge on the ancient world was unparalleled. By now she could very well be one of the world's leading experts.'

They ate their meals and turned in for the night. The *Lion's Mane* had fold-out beds in the living room and a curtain that gave each of them their own sleeping area.

The next few days passed slowly as they coasted across the continent. Down to Denmark, to Germany, Austria and over the Baltic States. It was much faster travelling by airship than over land, but it was still a long journey. By the time they reached Greece, their provisions were running dangerously low.

Mr Doyle moored the ship at the ancient city of Athens to resupply. Neither Jack nor Scarlet had visited before and they found it awe-inspiring. The city was a vast grid of narrow streets nestled around ancient hills and monuments. White buildings with red-tile roofs were crammed next to marble buildings. Columns topped with statues of Greek heroes speared up everywhere.

'What's that place on the hill?' Jack asked.

'The Acropolis,' Mr Doyle said. 'It's a citadel dating back to ancient times. There are many famous buildings in Greece. Possibly the most famous is the Parthenon.'

'Isn't that in Rome?'

'No, that's the *Pantheon*. The two are often confused,' Mr Doyle smiled. 'The Parthenon is a temple dedicated to the Goddess Athena.'

'She's known as the Goddess of Wisdom,' Scarlet said. 'Brinkie Buckeridge once fought a pitched battle in the Parthenon. She defeated fifty men with swords. All she had to defend herself was an umbrella and a poodle.'

'An umbrella and a…what?' Jack asked.

'It was a *very* vicious poodle.'

Jack knew better than to argue.

By the time they set off again, the sun was low in the sky and it was hot inside the *Lion's Mane*. Below lay the sea. Jack watched the passing islands with interest. They were like pieces of jewellery laid out on a sheet of shimmering glass. He could see small towns on many of them, but several looked uninhabited.

'There's a lot of islands down there,' he murmured.

'Thousands,' Mr Doyle said. 'Trying to find the right one is like finding a needle in a haystack.' He examined his map. 'I believe we are close, but it may take a few minutes to determine which one is Kasos.'

Mr Doyle continued to examine his map. Finally he gave a satisfied grunt and steered the airship towards a pair of sunbaked islands. The larger had hills running down its centre with small towns and connecting roads on either side. He aimed the *Lion's Mane* towards the southern end, bringing it in to land near a fishing port.

They disembarked, tying the *Lion's Mane* to a nearby

railing. An elderly man came out of his house and Mr Doyle spoke to him in Greek before handing over a few coins.

'It seems we must pay for parking,' the detective said. 'Not an unreasonable request.'

'Was he able to tell you anything about Miss Carfax?' Jack asked.

He nodded. 'She is quite well known. She has a house on the shoreline about a mile west of here.'

They followed a path around the coast. The ground was dry and rocky with scattered scrub clinging to the hills. Far below, the sea was clear and clean; a sailing boat moved across the shimmering water. Jack hoped they might be able to find accommodation; the bunks on board the *Lion's Mane* were fine, but nothing like sleeping in a real bed.

Jack spotted a large white house up the hill. It had two storeys and a flat roof except for a circular dome, painted blue, at the rear. The doors were azure with turquoise frames. Potted plants, crowded with flowers, hung along the walls. Wide awnings protected the windows.

A small steamer lay moored in the harbour below. Mr Doyle quickened his pace.

'I don't like the look of that vessel,' he said.

'They may only be tourists,' Scarlet said.

'We'll see.'

As they walked up the driveway to the front door, Jack heard a high-pitched scream from inside.

Mr Doyle pulled out his gun and threw himself at the door.

'Take your hands off that woman!' he shouted.

CHAPTER TWELVE

A man with blond hair slowly swung a machine gun towards Mr Doyle. 'That's a very nice revolver,' he said. 'I suggest you put it down before you hurt yourself.'

'You will be the ones surrendering your weapons,' Mr Doyle said. 'The authorities will be here within seconds.'

Another man with a scar running down the side of his face had a gun trained on a woman with greying hair. Presumably, she was Phoebe Carfax. A black-haired man had his weapon pointed at an elderly Greek maid tied to a chair.

A glance passed between Blondie and Scar Face.

'I don't believe you,' Scar Face said. 'You're lying.'

'You don't have to believe me,' Mr Doyle replied. 'Lower your weapons and no-one will be hurt.'

'Pain may be unavoidable,' Black Hair said.

'Jack,' Mr Doyle said. 'Release the lady that these men have so impolitely tied to that chair.'

'Don't move.'

Black Hair waved his machine gun at Jack. It was cool in the darkening room, lit now by two oil lamps on the mantelpiece, but a trickle of sweat slid down Jack's cheek.

Mr Doyle cocked his head. 'Ah,' he said. 'That sounds like the police.'

Black Hair looked to his companions. At the same moment, Mr Doyle grabbed Jack and Scarlet, dragging them behind a stone table. Then he fired twice at the lamps and they exploded, scattering fire across the room. Black Hair fired the machine gun back, razing the wall behind them.

'They're over there, officers!' Mr Doyle cried. 'Shoot! Shoot!'

The two men shot at the open door and Mr Doyle rolled out from behind the table. In the flickering light he was more like a ghost than a man. He crossed the room in an instant. Phoebe swung about, elbowing Blondie in the stomach, just as Mr Doyle reached Black Hair and knocked him out with a single blow.

Jack heard a sound from behind. Climbing to his feet, he saw the silhouettes of men, armed with machine guns, racing up the path.

Somehow I don't think they're the police.

He threw himself at the door, slamming it shut, and jammed an armchair under the handle. Scarlet crept over to him.

'Not wanting more visitors?' she asked.

'I'm a party pooper,' he said. The door shuddered as men hammered against it.

Scarlet grabbed Jack's arm. 'Come on,' she said. 'Move! Those men have guns!'

They scrambled towards Mr Doyle and Phoebe Carfax. The detective had disposed of Scar Face and was now engaged in a fistfight with Blondie. Phoebe snatched up a candlestick, swung it like a baseball bat, and the man slipped senseless to the ground.

Bullets smashed through the timber door. Jack and Scarlet went to help the maid, who was struggling to remove her bonds. Now she finally broke loose, but cried out as another wave of bullets sliced through the door. She fell in a heap.

Mr Doyle fired a few warning shots at the doorway as Phoebe rushed over. 'Oh my God,' she moaned. 'Sophie's dead.'

'I'm sorry, my dear,' Mr Doyle said.

The flames were spreading from the shattered lamps, jumping to the curtains and licking the ceiling.

'Not another burning building,' Jack said.

'Looks like it,' Scarlet said.

'We need to get out of here,' Phoebe Carfax said. 'We can go out the back door.'

'That won't be safe,' Mr Doyle said. 'They'll be expecting us.'

'Then let's try upstairs.'

Phoebe picked up one of the machine guns. Another hail of bullets reduced the front door to matchsticks, the chair fell away and silhouetted figures appeared. Phoebe opened fire.

Scarlet started, 'This reminds me of a Brinkie book where—'

'Not now, Scarlet,' Jack said.

At the top of the stairs, Mr Doyle hesitated.

'Where to now?'

'I thought you were in charge,' Phoebe said.

'Isn't there another way out?'

'Same old Ignatius Doyle. Still as impulsive as ever.'

Jack and Scarlet exchanged glances. That didn't sound like Mr Doyle at all.

Footsteps came from below. Mr Doyle herded Jack, Scarlet and Phoebe into the nearest room, locking the door as Phoebe headed towards a painting. Jack noticed for the first time that she dressed like a man, in brown trousers and a blue shirt.

What an incredible woman, he thought.

'Now isn't the time to admire the art,' Mr Doyle said.

Something exploded downstairs. The fire must have really taken hold. The door handle turned, followed by a shot into the lock. Mr Doyle returned fire and somebody cried out on the other side.

Tilting the painting, Phoebe revealed a safe embedded

in the wall. Unlocking it, she removed a shining brass cylinder.

'Good heavens,' Scarlet said.

'The Broken Sun,' Jack breathed.

'Only part of it,' Phoebe said with a quick smile. 'But still one of the greatest finds ever to come out of the ancient world.'

Mr Doyle had been peering out the window. 'Here's our exit!' he said. 'Quickly!'

Phoebe, Jack and Scarlet followed him through a pair of French doors onto a small balcony. An awning hung below.

'You can't expect me to jump onto that,' Phoebe said. 'It's not safe!'

'And staying here with a gang of killers is?' Mr Doyle lifted Phoebe into his arms. 'Let's go!'

He launched himself over the side.

Jack and Scarlet followed a moment later, bouncing off the awning and landing on a bulky mass.

Oof!

'Well done!' Mr Doyle cried.

They had landed on one of the criminals, knocking him out cold!

The house was now fully alight. They ran down the path to a steamcar with its engine running. Mr Doyle climbed behind the wheel, the others piling into the back. Jack and Scarlet quickly introduced themselves to Phoebe as they roared down the road. But she was hardly listening. She gave a small cry as she looked back at her burning home.

Mr Doyle glanced over his shoulder. 'I'm so sorry about your house,' he said.

'I'm sure you're not!' she snapped. 'And it isn't the first time you've burnt down my home.' She turned to Jack and Scarlet. 'Does he do that a lot? Reduce buildings to ashes.'

'It does happen a bit,' Scarlet admitted.

Jack was more intrigued by Phoebe's other comment. 'When did Mr Doyle burn down your house?'

'At least we've escaped,' Mr Doyle interrupted.

'Except for dear Sophie,' Phoebe said, wiping away a tear. 'She was a loyal employee and a friend.'

Jack looked out at the dark sky. He began to breathe a little easier. They just needed to get back to the *Lion's Mane*. He caught a glimpse of the moon—a brilliant round globe in the sky—and then it was blotted out. Something slammed into the steamcar's roof, almost knocking them off the road. Mr Doyle cursed, struggling for control.

A small airship had swiped the top of their vehicle. Jack watched in horror as it made a sharp turn and zoomed towards them once more.

'Look out!' he cried.

The airship slammed into their vehicle again. Mr Doyle swerved, fighting to steer it back to the centre of the moonlit road. He passed a machine gun back to Phoebe.

'See if you can stop them,' he yelled.

Phoebe pushed Jack aside, leaned out the window, braced the weapon against her shoulder and fired. The airship crashed into the roof of their car again.

'The gondola is metal,' she yelled. 'I can't penetrate it.'

'Fire at the balloon!' ordered Mr Doyle.

'Is that safe?' Scarlet asked.

Airship balloons were filled with hydrogen. Bullets might cause it to burst into flame, crash into their car and kill them all.

'We'll be fine,' the detective said. 'I think.'

Phoebe fired a few more rounds. The car was hit again, this time almost tipping over. Jack and Scarlet grabbed Phoebe around the waist to stop her from flying out. They dragged her inside.

'Thank you,' she said. 'But we now have another problem.'

'What's that?' Mr Doyle asked, zigzagging the steamcar about the road to avoid their attackers. 'Is it another airship?'

'I dropped the machine gun.'

'*What?*'

'No-one could have held on to it!' she snapped. 'I almost fell out of the car!'

'This is no time for an argument,' Jack said, glancing at Scarlet. He was beginning to understand why these two hadn't spoken in years. 'I think the airship's—'

The steamcar was hit again, but this time Mr Doyle couldn't keep them on the road. The car shot across a rocky, uneven field. A grappling hook speared through the rear passenger window, sending glass everywhere as it sunk into the roof like a hook catching a fish. It had come from the airship. The car began to tilt off the ground.

Jack cried out as he crashed into Scarlet.

They're trying to upend us.

'Get ready to jump!' Mr Doyle yelled.

'What?' Phoebe cried. 'From a moving vehicle?'

'They'll have us in a second!'

'But…but…'

'Get ready to jump and roll!'

'Look!' Scarlet cried.

The shimmering sea lay ahead. Mr Doyle was driving them directly towards a cliff. 'Almost there!' he yelled. 'And now…jump!'

Phoebe pushed the door open and leapt with a curse. Scarlet disappeared through the opposite door. Jack followed, hitting the ground hard, but rolling as his parents had taught him in the circus. He caught sight of Mr Doyle making a similar exit.

The car flew off the cliff, the spear still attached, and plummeted towards the sea, dragging the airship down with it.

'Run!' Mr Doyle yelled.

The rear end of the airship slammed into the cliff face, missing them by inches. There was a large tearing sound as it flipped over the side and crashed into the rocks below.

Wa-oophf!

The hydrogen ignited, turning night into day.

Jack shielded his eyes, joining the others as they carefully made their way back to the edge. The heat was immense as the hydrogen burned away. The rocky shore lay fifty feet below. What remained of the airship was broken and smouldering, the ribs of the balloon like the bones of a beached whale. The steamcar had also torn apart and was now fully ablaze.

Phoebe Carfax started down the slope.

'My dear,' Mr Doyle said. 'What are you doing?'

'What does it look like?' She cast him an exasperated glance. 'The other pieces of the Broken Sun may be aboard the airship.'

Mr Doyle sighed, turning to Jack and Scarlet.

'She may need some assistance,' Scarlet said.

'Phoebe has always been able to look after herself,' Ignatius Doyle said. 'Still, there may be some clues to be found.'

After ordering Jack and Scarlet to stay on the cliff, Mr Doyle and Phoebe examined the remains of the car. They disappeared into the shattered compartment of the airship's gondola, emerging a few minutes later with a bag. They scrambled up the slope.

Phoebe's face was aglow with excitement. 'We have them,' she said breathlessly. 'The other pieces of the Broken Sun. With these we will find New Atlantis!'

Mr Doyle was less excited. 'We still don't know who owned the airship. No-one on board survived the crash. And the men carried no identification. We are indeed lucky that the bag containing the artefact was not destroyed in the crash.'

'Imagine that,' Scarlet said. 'Atlantis.'

'*New* Atlantis,' Jack corrected her.

'And still a myth until I see evidence,' Mr Doyle said.

'Which I hope to provide,' Phoebe said. 'Once we sit down to properly examine the artefact.'

'I suggest returning to my residence in London,' Mr Doyle said to Phoebe. 'I doubt anywhere in Greece would be safe right now.'

'I'm not sure we're safe anywhere at all,' Phoebe said. 'But your place is as good as any.'

They walked back to the village where the locals had been roused by the airship's explosion. One of the shop owners promised Phoebe that the authorities would be summoned and a decent burial arranged for Sophie.

After boarding the *Lion's Mane*, Jack stoked the engine, asking Mr Doyle if he had discovered anything else aboard the wrecked airship or car.

'Surprisingly little,' the detective admitted. 'The men were well built and heavily tattooed. I suspect they were mercenaries.'

'There was nothing to indicate the owner of the car, either,' Phoebe said.

'Their employer must be rich,' Mr Doyle said. 'And have international connections. Not everyone could afford such an operation—or know whom to hire.'

'There was a boat in the harbour when we arrived,' Scarlet said.

'It wasn't there when we left. I suspect they took off when they realised their plans had gone awry.'

Jack turned to Phoebe. 'Do you know anyone who would kill to find New Atlantis?'

'Only every archaeologist on the planet,' Phoebe sighed. 'No, I'm exaggerating. Most archaeologists don't believe it ever existed. But its discovery *would* be the greatest archaeological find in history.'

'What do you think?' Scarlet asked. 'Do you really believe it existed?'

'Oh yes. Every piece of evidence I've accumulated over the years indicates it was real, and years ahead of its time.'

'I'll believe it when I see it,' Mr Doyle said.

'If you're not interested in Atlantis,' Phoebe said, 'then why are you here?'

Mr Doyle did not immediately answer. 'I have a separate investigation,' he said. 'It has intersected with your own.'

They were ready for departure. With the mooring ropes cast off, the *Lion's Mane* climbed into the sky. Looking back over the darkened island, they saw a small fire burning ferociously.

'That's my home,' Phoebe said. 'Or it was.'

'I'm so sorry, my dear,' Mr Doyle said.

Phoebe sighed, turning to Jack and Scarlet. 'Has he told you how he burnt down my other home?'

Mr Doyle tutted. 'That was hardly a residence.'

'I *lived* there!'

'It was the gardener's cottage at Oxford,' Mr Doyle explained. 'Although, admittedly, Phoebe was living there at the time.'

'And you burnt it down?' Scarlet said.

Phoebe turned to the detective. 'Really, Ignatius. What sort of impression have you given your young assistants?'

The detective was suddenly very busy examining the airship's console. 'It was a long time ago,' he said. 'It must have slipped my mind.'

'Is that like the country of Norway slipping my mind?' Jack asked.

Phoebe continued before Mr Doyle could reply. 'Your employer was quite a scoundrel at Oxford,' she said. 'A very naughty boy.'

Jack and Scarlet exchanged glances.

Mr Doyle? A very naughty boy?

Impossible!

CHAPTER THIRTEEN

'England!' Mr Doyle said. 'Glorious England!'

It seemed like a hundred years had passed since they had left. Now the sun creased the horizon as they neared the coastline.

Mr Doyle prepared a small meal of tinned kippers and vegetables while Phoebe Carfax made tea. At first, Jack had thought Phoebe to be bad-tempered, but he soon realised that what appeared to be a difficult personality was in fact a wicked sense of humour.

'We'll need to work on that hair now we're returning to civilisation,' Phoebe told Jack, producing a comb from nowhere. 'I've seen bird's nests that are more orderly.'

'I'm always talking to Jack about his hair,' Scarlet

grinned. As usual, her own was brushed, flowing as smoothly as a stream in spring. 'I check it occasionally for insects. There was a preying mantis in there once.'

Phoebe wrestled Jack's hair into submission. 'That's not true,' he protested. 'It was a grasshopper—and a small one at that!'

When they were sitting around the dining table to eat, Phoebe told them she looked forward to trying to crack the code contained within the Broken Sun.

Mr Doyle made a *harrump,* spearing a kipper with his fork.

'Mock me all you want, Ignatius,' Phoebe said. 'All the evidence points to it.'

'Rumours do not count as evidence.'

'Place a blind man in a room with a vase and he is able to determine it is pottery.'

'But a blind man may also mistake the tail of an elephant for a snake.'

Phoebe placed the pieces of the Broken Sun on a bench. It was strange seeing them together, three golden batons with turning dials decorated with a myriad of pictures.

'That's neither a snake nor an elephant,' she said. 'It's the most highly advanced piece of technology ever to come out of the ancient world—and it's evidence that Atlantis existed. It will lead us to New Atlantis.'

They continued towards London. Mr Doyle veered the *Lion's Mane* into a lane of city-bound airships, and soon the ship was descending to the roof of 221 Bee Street.

Gloria greeted them as they climbed down to the balcony. They introduced Phoebe and the women shook hands cordially.

'You're in charge of looking after Ignatius, are you?' Phoebe said. 'That must be quite a challenge.'

'Mostly I keep him under control by hitting him with a stick.'

'Has anything of a pressing nature arisen?' Mr Doyle asked Gloria.

'Just the usual range of murders, muggings and thefts.'

'Good.' When Mr Doyle asked for an update on the condition of Professor Clarke, it turned out the man had still not arisen from his sleep.

'Would you be so kind as to put up the out-of-office sign?' Mr Doyle asked. 'And locking the front door?'

'Are we expecting trouble?' Gloria asked.

'Possibly.'

Jack showed Phoebe to the guest bedroom and gave her a tour of the apartment. It took longer than expected as there were some places he had never been to himself. Phoebe was both bemused and amazed by the mayhem.

'Ignatius hasn't changed,' she said. 'Still as messy as ever.'

Jack felt defensive. 'He has solved many mysteries.'

'I would imagine a good detective would want to find Atlantis.'

'I think he's more interested in finding his son.' As soon as the words were out of Jack's mouth, he regretted them.

'What do you mean?'

'I shouldn't have said anything.'

But the horse had already bolted. Jack explained briefly what had brought them to this point in the investigation.

'He was certain Phillip had been killed in the war,' Jack concluded. 'Until now.'

Phoebe swallowed. 'That's so distressing,' she said. 'I've watched and admired Ignatius' achievements from afar, but I didn't know about his son. It must be terrible not knowing if he's alive or dead.'

'Mr Doyle's a great man,' Jack said. 'And a brilliant detective.'

'I'm sure he is,' Phoebe said, gently. 'Mind you, he probably would have been a better archaeologist.'

An archaeologist? Jack tried to imagine Mr Doyle poking about an ancient ruin in a foreign country. It was not that strange an idea. They returned to the dining room where cups of Mr Doyle's famous hot chocolate were waiting on the table.

The room was the only place in the apartment that contained any free space. A twelve-seat table was in the middle. It was an ancient, solid oak construction that Mr Doyle had said once belonged to Alfred the Great. The room had no windows, only a skylight directly over the table.

Stacked against the walls were Mr Doyle's collections of tin cans, framed bus tickets, wind-up toys, comic books and prosthetic limbs.

'Nice to see you've finally found a place for those wooden legs,' Phoebe said.

'Have you always collected things, Mr Doyle?' Jack asked.

The detective smiled. 'I don't think of myself as a collector,' he said, checking his revolver as the others drank. 'Things just look better grouped together.'

'Are you worried they'll try to steal the Broken Sun again?' Scarlet asked, eyeing the weapon.

'I'm planning on it. Their capture will lead us to their employer and to whoever sent Amelia the watch.'

'The watch?' Phoebe asked.

'I will explain later,' he said. 'I suggest we turn in for the night. An addled brain will not function.'

After Scarlet had retired, Jack lingered for one last look at the Broken Sun. The pieces still made no sense. As he left to weave through the mounds of odd possessions, he turned to see Phoebe sitting across from the detective. She placed a gentle hand on Mr Doyle's arm.

'Tell me about your son,' she said.

Back in his room, Jack dressed for bed. Bertha's cage was in his chamber. Jack fed her, turned out his light and settled in to stare at the ceiling. The last few days had been exhausting. They had travelled halfway around the world and were still no closer to discovering the truth about Mr Doyle's son.

How does this whole mystery fit together?

It had begun with the watch being delivered to

Amelia Doyle. Then the warning note about the British Museum. Professor Clarke—the real man—had been assaulted with a sleeping poison. And all this had led them on a search for the Broken Sun.

But what was the connection between the Broken Sun and the watch? And how did Phillip Doyle fit into all this?

The next morning, Jack woke to a knock. Mr Doyle's head appeared in the doorway.

'Rise and shine, my boy,' he said. 'We're out here unravelling the mysteries of the universe.'

'Really?' Jack said, struggling out of bed.

'No. Actually, I'm about to make breakfast. Food for the body provides energy for the mind!'

Jack had eaten Mr Doyle's cooking on a few occasions. While the great detective had many abilities, cooking was not one of them. As Jack wandered into the kitchen, Mr Doyle was already rummaging through one of the cabinets.

'Oh dear,' he said, after a minute. 'We seem to be down to half a loaf of mouldy bread and a piece of cheese so hard you could write with it.'

'I did mention that we needed to shop,' Gloria said, arching an eyebrow. 'Once a month is not nearly enough.'

'Possibly we should delay breakfast and we'll spend some time examining the Broken Sun.' Dust exploded as he closed the cupboard. 'Gloria, would you be so kind as to retrieve it from the safe?'

Gloria disappeared in the direction of the library.

The safe was built into a space behind one of its many bookcases.

'I must remember to buy food more frequently,' Mr Doyle said. 'I once survived for a year solely on marmalade and gherkins. It was while I was investigating a case involving a rubber brain, a hairdresser and a singing turtle—'

A scream echoed through the apartment.

'Good Lord!' Mr Doyle cried.

'That was Gloria!' Scarlet said.

They tore along the hallway to find her lying face-down on the floor with a purple thorn beside her.

'No!' Jack said. 'She's been poisoned!'

A sound came from the balcony. Jack charged towards it with Mr Doyle close behind, and they saw a small, dark-haired man disappearing over the railing. In his hand was the bag containing the pieces of the Broken Sun.

CHAPTER FOURTEEN

But Jack didn't care about the Broken Sun.

Gloria was the closest thing he had to a mother, and now she might die. Jack peered over the balcony. The man was nimbly climbing down the side of the building. He was already halfway to the street, the bag slung effortlessly over his shoulder.

Jack had been an acrobat, but he would ever have attempted something so risky. A small external elevator clung to the side of the building. Little more than a simple pulley system, Mr Doyle and the team used the odd-looking contraption to reach the street quickly.

'Jack!' Mr Doyle cried. 'Wait—'

But Jack ignored him, releasing a lever and shooting

to the bottom. The dark-haired man was already turning the corner.

A light morning fog floated about the streets. The man raced ahead, darting around horse-drawn carriages and steamcars. He disappeared into the mist of a Stevenson 77. Jack followed, almost colliding with a delivery man with an armful of parcels.

'Sorry!' Jack yelped.

'Blasted young—'

Jack heard no more. The assailant was ahead of him, slowed by the morning crowds. They were heading into the centre of London, the shopping district clotted with department stores.

Then Jack lost sight of him.

No!

Jack reached Blessington's department store, one of the largest in London, with more than fifty levels and dozens of elevators. *He must have gone inside.* Hurrying up the steam-powered escalator, Jack soon found himself in the men's clothing and accessories section. He spent several minutes searching the floor before heading up to the next. A hand grabbed his shoulder from behind.

Phoebe Carfax.

'Where is he?' she asked.

'I don't know. Somewhere on this floor.'

Peering over a display of hats, Jack spotted the man heading towards the elevators at the far end.

'We'll need backup,' Phoebe said. 'Ignatius and Scarlet aren't far behind. You go back and I'll follow him.'

'No,' Jack said. 'I'll follow him.' Nothing was going to stop him from catching the man. 'You let Scarlet and Mr Doyle know what's happening.'

Phoebe looked like she wanted to argue, but something in Jack's face told her she would be wasting her time.

Jack watched the man approach the elevator and step inside. The floor dial raced up to the number '12'.

Waiting for it to return, Jack climbed in and hit the button. Disquiet swam in his stomach. Was the man really on a shopping spree after stealing the Broken Sun? What was he doing on the twelfth floor?

And what's so special about this elevator?

The interior was old, the walls covered with timber panelling, and there was a handrail at waist height. Jack's eyes focused on a mark halfway up the wall. It almost looked like...

...a shoe print.

When the elevator reached the twelfth floor, it emitted a puff of steam and the doors slid open. Two men started to enter, but Jack waved them back.

'Building's on fire,' he said. 'Take the stairs, please.'

He slapped the button marked 'G' and the doors shut. A trapdoor in the ceiling was ajar and, as the elevator was descending, Jack placed a foot on the handrail and pushed himself up until his hand caught the edge of the hatch. Shoving it out of the way, he climbed onto the roof of the moving cabin.

A line of twenty elevators slid up and down like cogs

in a mighty machine. They all moved at various speeds, stopping and starting, their hoisting ropes trembling in the gas-lit interior. Jack coughed. Steam choked the air.

The elevator slowed and stopped. Glancing back through the hatch, Jack saw an elderly woman enter. She did not look up.

Who would?

The elevator started to climb. It was only at the last moment that Jack looked up to see the man slamming into him like a cannonball, sending him flying off the roof into midair.

Jack landed on the roof of the next elevator, narrowly missing the cable. The man leapt down and Jack rolled out of the way. The bag containing the pieces of the Broken Sun was nowhere to be seen.

Scrambling to his feet, Jack threw a punch—and missed. The man shifted his stance, dropped and aimed low with a sweeping kick, knocking Jack's legs from under him. The elevator started to ascend as Jack threw himself at his assailant in a wild attack, forcing him backwards. They teetered, wrestling at the edge of the roof, clouds of steam and open space beyond. The man tried to twist sideways, but Jack headbutted him, pushing with all his might.

Smash!

They had slammed onto the roof of the next elevator. Jack heard one of the man's ribs crack, but it did not stop him. He flipped Jack over his head. Stepping back a few feet, he ran at Jack...

...and jumped right over him.

Jack spun about to see him fly over the next elevator and land on the one beyond. The man did not land neatly, sprawling untidily into the cabling. The elevator on the other side ascended and the man readied himself to cross to it.

Damn! He's going to escape.

Jack braced himself to jump too, but his legs were shaking. The man was now two elevators over with the elevator between them descending like a rock.

It's now or never.

Jack thought of Gloria, remembering her sightless eyes. He gritted his teeth and leapt, arms spiralling to drive him forward. He hit the edge, teetering perilously before regaining his balance.

He was too late. The thief leapt to the next chamber, carrying him out of sight.

No!

The man's elevator was heading up while Jack's was heading down.

Jack glanced behind him. There was no time to think. He took a running jump, leapt to the elevator behind him and the one beyond. The elevator zoomed up.

He peered over the side, his heart pounding like a bass drum. He was high up now, a hundred feet from the bottom. The thief was three elevators across and waiting for the one next to him to descend.

Jack took a single ragged breath and ran. Jumped. Crossed two elevators and hit the third one—hard, twisting his ankle. The pain was terrible, but Jack now found himself face to face with the man.

'Infidel! You will never find Atlantis.'

'I don't care about Atlantis!' Jack cried. 'You poisoned my friend. I want the antidote.'

'Never!'

The man sunk a fist into Jack's stomach, winding him, and followed it with a blinding jab. Jack saw stars.

'The location of New Atlantis has remained a secret for centuries,' he heard the man say. 'Did you really think you would find it?'

'I just want a cure for my friend,' Jack grunted.

'Your friend will sleep forever—as will you.'

I was stupid, Jack thought. *I should have waited for the others. And now Gloria will be lost.*

The man tipped Jack over the side. Jack grabbed the edge, held on tight. He looked up, silently imploring the man. But the eyes staring back were cold.

'Goodbye, boy.'

He brought his heel down onto Jack's fingers.

CHAPTER FIFTEEN

Craaack!

A shot rang out, cutting across the sound of machinery.

'No,' the thief gasped.

He staggered backwards. Blood began to dribble from the hole in the middle of his chest. He took another faltering step before plunging off the elevator.

Someone jumped onto the roof and reached for Jack.

'Hang on,' Scarlet cried. 'I've got you.'

She was just in time. Jack was ready to fade into unconsciousness. When the elevator slid to a halt, the trapdoor opened and Mr Doyle appeared, grabbing Jack's other hand.

'Are you all right, my boy?'

Jack could not reply. Everything turned to shadows as he was manhandled through the trapdoor and onto a stretcher. Racks of men's clothing flashed by, then there was darkness.

When he next woke, Jack found himself in a small gas-lit room. He gingerly felt his face. He had bruises everywhere and his jaw was swollen. Where was he?

'My boy?'

Mr Doyle was sitting in the shadows.

'You must stay in bed,' he said when Jack struggled to sit up. 'Doctor's orders.'

'Where am I?' Jack croaked. 'What time is it?'

'You're in hospital and it is morning.'

'The Broken Sun,' Jack said. 'And Gloria—'

'We have retrieved the Broken Sun,' Mr Doyle said. 'There was a bag secreted in an alcove in the elevator shaft. It appears the thief was using the area as some kind of home.'

The door eased open.

'Jack?' Scarlet appeared. 'Are you all right?'

Bursting into tears, she hugged him tightly. It hurt, but it was worth it. Almost.

'Did you really jump from that elevator?' Jack asked her. 'Or did I just imagine that?'

'She did,' Mr Doyle said, frowning. 'If I'd known she was going to do that, I wouldn't have allowed her through the trapdoor.'

'It's a good thing she did,' Jack said. 'I couldn't

hold on any longer.' He turned back to Scarlet. 'Bubbly Blinkingbutt would be proud.'

'Brinkie Buckeridge,' she said. 'And you're welcome.'

'And Gloria,' he said. 'Is she…?'

'Unconscious.' The detective let out a deep sigh. 'Asleep in the same manner as Professor Clarke.'

'I have to see her.'

'You must rest.'

'No.'

Mr Doyle gave in, helping Jack out the door. They all weaved up a flight of stairs to the next floor where Mr Doyle opened a door to reveal Gloria on a bed, staring up at the ceiling, her eyes half-open.

She looked like something dead.

Jack took her hand and tried to speak. 'We're here,' he finally said, his voice cracking. 'Mr Doyle, Scarlet and I are here.'

He started crying. He could not help it. After a time, he turned to Mr Doyle and said, 'Is she going to be all right?'

'The doctors have not been able to wake her,' Mr Doyle said. 'But we must do what we can. We must focus on the future.'

'What future? If we don't find a cure then Gloria's going to…'

He could not say it.

Then Gloria's going to die.

The tears began again. Scarlet's eyes were leaking too. The detective led them from the room. 'Have you ever known me to give up?' he asked.

Jack shook his head.

'Then I am certainly not giving up on Gloria,' he said. 'I will do everything in my power to find a cure. I have another friend at the British Museum, an expert in botany. He may be able to identify the thorn.'

'I doubt it,' Phoebe Carfax said, appearing in the hallway. 'But I may be able to help you. There are many ancient legends concerning Atlantis. One of them refers to a plant known as the Sleeping Death.'

'I'm not sure legends and myths will help us,' Mr Doyle said tightly.

Phoebe ignored him. 'The Sleeping Death produces a purple thorn. If stabbed, a person lapses into a sleep from which they may never recover.' She held up her hand as Scarlet sobbed. 'But the same plant also provides an antidote. Its ivory-coloured leaves, when ingested, are said to wake the sleeper.'

'So the same plant is both the poison,' Jack said, working through this revelation aloud, 'and the cure?'

'Exactly.'

They returned to Bee Street. Jack and Scarlet wanted to go with Mr Doyle to the British Museum, but the detective insisted they remain at the apartment. The pieces of the Broken Sun were hidden in the safe.

Jack, Scarlet and Phoebe made certain every window and door was locked. Jack settled at a small desk in the corner of the living room and tried to resume work on a jigsaw puzzle of Salvador Dalí's painting, *The Persistence of Memory*. Phoebe leafed through books in the library while Scarlet reread one of her Brinkie Buckeridge novels.

Jack stared sightlessly at the puzzle and tried to reconstruct the events of the last few days. Phillip Doyle's watch. Elevators. The Broken Sun. Black-haired assailants. None of it made any sense.

He lifted his head. He'd fallen asleep. Pieces of puzzle were stuck to his face. He pried them off, blearily looking about. Judging by the light, most of the day had passed. Voices were coming from the sitting room. He entered and could immediately tell that the detective had not been successful.

'The man I met with was one of the top experts in his field,' Mr Doyle was saying when Jack walked in. 'He said the thorn was from *Rosaceae*—the rose family—but he had never seen one like it.'

'Then what will we do?' Scarlet asked. 'We can't find the cure if we can't find the plant.'

Mr Doyle nodded glumly. 'I also visited a doctor friend of mine and described the situation,' he continued. 'He likened the effects to the paralysis caused by some snake bites that leave the victim aware of their surroundings, unable to communicate with those around them.'

'So Gloria and Professor Clarke are conscious,' Scarlet said, horrified. 'But unable to move?'

'What will we do?' Jack asked.

'We can do something,' Phoebe said, her eyes shrewd. 'There is a way we can locate a cure.'

'What are you suggesting?' Mr Doyle asked.

'It is very simple,' Phoebe said. 'We must find New Atlantis.'

Mr Doyle scowled. 'You're suggesting we find a mythical city that has been missing for ten thousand years?'

'I am.'

'And you believe we can succeed where so many others have failed?'

'They did not have the Broken Sun,' Phoebe pointed out. 'We do. And we have evidence that New Atlantis exists.'

'You are referring to...?'

'The thorn.'

'I have solved many baffling mysteries,' Mr Doyle murmured. 'But this is one of the strangest.'

'Strange is the name of the game,' Jack said. 'You told me that once.'

'I did.' Mr Doyle nodded. 'All right, we have a hypothesis. Now we need to test it.'

'The best way to do that is to crack the code of the Broken Sun,' Phoebe said.

Mr Doyle sighed. 'At least that may move us forward,' he said. 'I'll retrieve it from the safe.'

Minutes later they were in the dining room with the three cylindrical pieces spread over the table. But when they tried them together, the ends would not fit.

Scarlet picked up a piece and tried rattling it while Mr Doyle examined another piece, holding it up like a telescope.

'Have you been able to decipher any of the letters?' Jack asked Phoebe. 'They're all Greek to me.'

'I wish they were Greek,' Phoebe responded. 'It would be easier to understand. The only characters I can see on here are in Ancient Sumerian. And they appear to be numbers.'

'Hmm,' Mr Doyle grunted. 'It's like putting a jigsaw puzzle together without the original picture.'

'This will sound strange,' Scarlet said, examining one of the panels. 'But this looks like the bottom of India.'

'What?' Phoebe asked. She examined the artefact. 'I think you're right. And that could be Sri Lanka. And Italy.'

They all grouped around the cylinders to examine them again in earnest, searching for sections that resembled parts of the world. Several more were found, but after two hours they sat back in frustration.

'It would seem that sections of the world map have been placed onto the metal dials,' Mr Doyle said. 'But there's no clear way to tell how they fit together.'

'Maybe it's been damaged,' said Scarlet.

'It doesn't appear damaged,' Phoebe said. 'But we're obviously missing a vital piece of the puzzle.' She sighed. 'We need a new perspective on this. What's the best way to do that?'

'What about examining the panels with our goggles?' Jack suggested.

'A closer magnification,' Mr Doyle said. 'That's an excellent idea.'

Jack found sets of goggles for everyone. Another hour passed and Jack placed his piece down, scratching his head.

'I'm going cross-eyed,' Scarlet said. 'There are pieces of maps, but also stars, waves and odd letters. None of it makes any sense.'

'We may be over-thinking this,' Phoebe said.

'What do you mean?' Mr Doyle asked.

'Maybe there's another question we should be asking ourselves. Why, for example, are there twenty-seven dials?'

'Twenty-seven,' Jack mused. 'What's so important about that number?'

'There are twenty-seven books in the New Testament,' Mr Doyle said. 'And twenty-seven letters in the Hebrew alphabet.'

'There are twenty-seven channels of communication with God in the Kabbalah,' Phoebe said.

'And twenty-seven bones in the human hand,' Scarlet added.

Jack said, 'And twenty-seven is…Well, it's bigger than twenty-six and less than twenty-eight.'

'Mozart wrote twenty-seven concertos for piano and orchestra,' Scarlet pointed out. 'The second movement of Number Twenty in D minor is definitely the best.'

'No doubt about that,' Jack sighed.

Phoebe's eyes were shining. 'That number may help us a great deal,' she said, spinning the dials on a piece of the Broken Sun. 'There is a blank square on every single dial. What if most of these must be made to line up, with only the number twenty-seven showing?'

'But there aren't any numbers on the Broken Sun,' Scarlet said.

'There are,' Phoebe said, pointing at a double arrow shape on one of the dials. She snatched up another piece and spun it around to an inscription in the shape of a shield. 'These are in Ancient Sumerian.'

Phoebe carefully turned each of the dials so that only the numbers representing two and seven were showing. Then she fit the sections together with the shorter piece in the middle. It snapped into a single shaft.

'I don't believe it,' Phoebe gasped. 'It's actually…'

Before she could continue, something clicked within the device. Phoebe put it down as it unfurled into a large sheet of metal, like a butterfly emerging from a cocoon and spreading its wings.

'Incredible,' Mr Doyle said.

'Good heavens,' Scarlet said.

'Bazookas,' Jack said, frowning. 'What does it mean?'

'I…I'm not sure,' Phoebe said. She picked up the metal sheet and turned it over. The dials were now a straight strip. 'I think each of them moves.'

They did. A single support ran across the back, but the strips could slide, lining the symbols up for any number of combinations.

'We seem to have moved ahead,' Mr Doyle said. 'But we still have some way to go.'

'So it would seem,' Phoebe said.

'Be kind to yourself,' Mr Doyle said. 'You've done better than anyone else in thousands of years.'

'But what do we do now?'

Jack touched the strips of metal. 'Some are locked in place.'

Phoebe tried moving them. 'You're right.'

'How many of them move?' Scarlet asked.

Jack tried them. 'Nine.'

'Is there a commonality between the pieces that move?' Mr Doyle asked.

'They *do* have something in common,' Phoebe said. 'They all have a star on them!'

'I believe you're correct,' Mr Doyle said. 'Do any of the legends regarding New Atlantis refer to stars?'

'Not directly,' Phoebe said. 'But the ancients were certainly interested in the constellations. Astronomy was quite advanced for its time.'

'I don't know anything about stars,' Jack said. 'Except that our sun is one of them.'

'The sun just happens to be the star closest to Earth,' Mr Doyle said.

Phoebe explained. 'Ancient civilisations created pictures from them—the constellations—Leo, Gemini and so forth. Most originated with the ancient Greeks.'

'What about the pictures the stars create?' Mr Doyle asked. 'A lion. A scorpion. Twins...'

'The only legend that relates directly to the Broken

Sun is that of Jason and the Argonauts. He was a hero of ancient Greek myth who searched for the Golden Fleece.' Phoebe paused. 'There's a story that Jason's hand will lead to his eternal twin. And his twin will lead to New Atlantis.'

'Is there a constellation for Jason?' Jack asked.

'No,' Phoebe said. 'But it is a legend that has always baffled Atlantis historians.' She frowned. 'Not all the constellations have survived. In fact… Ignatius, do you have a book of the skies?'

Within minutes she was leafing through a dusty tome.

'I thought so,' she cried. 'There *was* a constellation relating to Jason. It was *Argo Navis*.'

'*Argo Navis*?' Jack repeated the strange words.

'It was named after the ship used by Jason on his quest—the *Argo*. The constellation was enormous and it's the only one not to survive from Ptolemy's time. It was later broken up into four smaller constellations, each referring to a part of a ship,' Phoebe said.

'Keels have steered ships for centuries,' Mr Doyle said.

'The constellation *Carina* is the keel,' Phoebe said, excitedly. 'And it has nine main stars!'

She placed the book with the picture of the constellation next to the artefact. Then she arranged the stars so they resembled the picture. When she slotted the last star into place, another click came from the device. It was now locked in.

'That's it,' Phoebe said. 'The Broken Sun is complete.'

'Except it still doesn't seem to be pointing us anywhere,' Scarlet said.

They stood in silence. Finally Mr Doyle drew a sharp breath and took the device from Phoebe. He climbed onto a chair, holding the Broken Sun up high.

'Everyone has an eternal twin,' he said. 'You just need the right light to see them.'

Late afternoon sunshine shone through the skylight onto the Broken Sun, casting a shadow across the table. There was no mistaking it: the odd shape created a hazy map of the African continent. Two crisp, crisscrossing lines formed an 'X' off the north-west coast.

'My friends,' Mr Doyle said. 'We have found New Atlantis.'

CHAPTER SIXTEEN

'We're going on an expedition to a remote island in order to find a civilisation lost for ten thousand years,' Phoebe argued. 'It can't be done on a budget.'

It was morning and everyone was gathered on the top floor of 221 Bee Street. Mr Doyle, Jack, Scarlet and Phoebe Carfax were in the sitting room eating toast and jam, discussing their plans for the days ahead. Jack ate his meal quietly, but inside he was filled with a sense of hope. Gloria was still in hospital—an early morning messenger had reported no change in her condition—but now there was a chance of saving her.

'I'm not interested in lost civilisations,' Mr Doyle said. 'Only in finding a cure for Gloria and Professor Clarke.'

'The only way to do that is with a fully equipped expedition,' Phoebe said. 'To attempt this on our own would be completely foolhardy.'

'We have done very well so far.'

'Thanks to me.'

'Thanks to us all.'

'But this is beyond the resources of four people.'

'Surely the *Lion's Mane*—'

'Really?' Now Phoebe sounded angry. 'You think your little ship is capable of such a journey?'

'She is.' Mr Doyle paused to think. 'But a larger ship would be faster...'

'And safer. What would we do if we encountered trouble? We know our enemies are willing to kill for New Atlantis.'

Mr Doyle glanced at Jack and Scarlet. Jack knew he was worried about their safety. Looking at himself in the mirror that morning, he'd been shocked at the face peering back: swollen, his right eye almost black.

I may as well have been run over by a steamtruck, he'd thought glumly.

'Having a few more people on our side might be helpful,' Jack pointed out. 'It took all of us to crack the code of the Broken Sun.'

Mr Doyle asked Phoebe, 'What do you know of Tobias Bradstreet?'

'The millionaire? He's one of the world's foremost amateur archaeologists, his specialty being Atlantis. How do *you* know him?'

The detective described their meeting.

'Perfect,' Phoebe said. 'Our chances of success just tripled.'

'I don't know.' The detective shook his head. 'Involving a stranger on this voyage—'

'Mr Doyle,' Jack interrupted. 'We have to think of Gloria.'

'Of course. You're right.'

Twenty-four hours later they were in a steamcab approaching Plymouth Harbour. Mr Doyle and Phoebe had met with Tobias Bradstreet and he immediately agreed to an expedition, promising to get an airship ready.

The harbour was crowded. Steam and smoke filled the air, reducing visibility to a few feet. Airships were using their horns to avoid collisions.

Mr Doyle explained how this was one of the busiest ports in the country. 'Most of the journeys to Africa leave from here,' he said. 'And much of the trade from the continent enters through Plymouth.'

Jack confessed he did not know a lot about Africa.

'It's still an unknown continent,' Mr Doyle said. 'People journey there to make their fortune. Some of them do, but many fall victim to its dangers.'

'What dangers?' Jack said.

Phoebe laughed. 'Where do I start? Typhoid. Malaria. Cannibals. Poor drinking water. Wild animals. The heat...'

'Surely it can't be that bad. No-one would go.'

'It's fine as long as you're careful,' Phoebe said.

'I've been to Africa on three separate expeditions and I didn't lose a man. Or a woman.'

'You've been to Africa?' Mr Doyle looked at Phoebe in amazement.

'I had to do something with my life after you jilted me at the altar.'

It took Jack a moment to realise what Phoebe Carfax had said.

'*Altar? You mean you and Mr Doyle—*'

'Were to be married,' Phoebe confirmed.

'It was all a long time ago,' Mr Doyle mumbled. 'I was younger.'

'We all were.' Phoebe shook her head. 'It's extraordinary what a bottle of gin will do to a man.'

Scarlet's mouth fell open. 'You were getting married and you were *drunk?*'

'But the church was closed,' Phoebe said. 'Which was reasonable: it was, after all, three in the morning. Still, that didn't stop us from breaking in.'

Jack couldn't have been more surprised if Mr Doyle had told them he was the white rabbit from *Alice in Wonderland*.

'He wasn't always this stuffy.' Phoebe winked at Jack. 'Ignatius was quite fun once.'

Married? Jack thought. *Drunk? Breaking and entering a church? At three in the morning?*

Bazookas!

The steamcab arrived at the terminal. Mr Doyle led them through a maze of vehicles, porters with trunks, women with dogs, families and goods carriers.

'You needn't worry about Africa,' Scarlet said to Jack. 'Brinkie has been there many times.'

'That's a comfort.'

'The last time she went there was in *The Adventure of the Cannibal Cousin*.'

'The...what? You're telling me,' Jack said slowly, 'that Brinkie has a cousin who is a cannibal?'

'Not by choice. His name is Bartholomew Buckeridge. Lost in the jungle with a dozen friends, he was captured by a cannibal tribe and forced to play cards to decide who would be eaten.'

Jack shook his head. 'The things that happen when you're lost in the jungle.'

'The days passed until only Bartholomew and another man remained,' Scarlet continued. 'That's when Bartholomew realised the man had been cheating the whole time, keeping a spare ace of spades up his sleeve to win. There was a fight to the death and Bartholomew escaped, but realised the soup he had been eating contained the remains of his brother, Whipple.'

'How horrible.'

Scarlet nodded. 'Especially when Bartholomew remembers all the times he asked for seconds,' she said. 'He eventually goes on to write a cookbook, *What I Ate in Deepest, Darkest Africa*. It is not a bestseller.'

'I wonder why.'

They reached a hangar marked '1859' where they

found an impressive-looking airship with its name emblazoned on the side.

'The *Explorer*. At least it has an appropriate name.'

Jack had never seen anything like it. The ship had nine levels including the main deck. The underside resembled an eighteenth-century vessel except it was bronze-plated. Two masts topped with crow's nests pierced a long, sausage-shaped balloon. Propulsion jets from the steam engine protruded from its square stern.

Tobias Bradstreet marched down the gangplank to greet them. He showed a special interest in Phoebe. 'I've followed your work for years,' he gushed. 'It's a pleasure to finally meet you.'

'The pleasure is all mine. I'm sure this will be a successful collaboration.'

'My navigator has checked the coordinates of your location and pinpointed a landmass known as Smollett's Island.'

'That's an unusual name,' Phoebe said.

'Named for a ship that was wrecked on the nearby reef a century ago,' Mr Bradstreet explained. 'The waters around the island are treacherous.' He waved them aboard. 'The porters will bring your luggage. I'll introduce you to Captain Malone and the others.'

The ship had a cast-iron interior and sealable hatchways. Mr Bradstreet said that the *Explorer* could also operate as a seagoing vessel if the balloon failed. 'Even if the hull is compromised,' he added, 'the hatches can be closed off to stop the ship from sinking.'

'There don't seem to be many crew,' Jack said.

'We don't need many,' Bradstreet said.

'Correct me if I'm wrong,' Mr Doyle said. 'But I believe the *Explorer* used to be a freighter.'

Bradstreet looked impressed. 'In its previous life it transported spices from India to Britain. The hold now contains exploration equipment.'

They reached the bridge. At the bow, crew were examining dials on their consoles and consulting charts. Captain Malone stood at the steering wheel. He was a serious-looking man with a grey beard and large ears.

'I didn't know we were bringing a woman,' he said to Bradstreet after the introductions. 'And children.'

'Phoebe Carfax is a world expert on Atlantis,' Bradstreet snapped. 'We're lucky to have her. And these are Mr Doyle's assistants.'

'I am *the* foremost expert on Atlantis,' Phoebe told Captain Malone. 'And Jack and Scarlet are highly accomplished in their own right.' She gave him a thin smile. 'I promise we won't spill tea on your steering wheel or play tiddlywinks in the corridors.'

'I'm sure you won't,' Captain Malone said, taken aback. 'Just as long as the journey goes smoothly.'

Bradstreet introduced the first mate, a rather more affable man by the name of Reg Smythe.

'I've only just joined the crew,' he said, shaking hands. 'It's an honour to be part of such a prestigious expedition.'

Bradstreet gave a small nod. 'You were with the

Singleton expedition to Everest, I believe.'

'Indeed. We spent some time in Nepal.'

'So what did you think of the Goddess of the Earth?' Mr Doyle asked. 'Was she as beautiful as they say?'

Smythe hesitated. 'Even more beautiful.' He glanced back at Captain Malone. 'I had best return to my duties.'

The captain nodded. 'We're rather busy right now,' he said. 'Seeing as how we must be away by fourteen-hundred hours.'

'Of course,' said Bradstreet, tight-lipped. 'We'll speak at dinner.'

Jack could see he was annoyed by the surly nature of the captain. Bradstreet may have been the owner of the ship, but the person in charge was Captain Malone.

They reached the galley where a small group of swarthy men were assembled around a table. Their leader was a man by the name of Charles Spaulding, a muscle-bound individual, clean-shaven and ruddy.

His two companions, from the South Sea Islands, had darker complexions. Bradstreet introduced them as brothers, Kip and Tan.

'I notice you have recently been in Afghanistan,' Mr Doyle said to Spaulding.

The man laughed. 'How do you know that?'

'The tattoo on your inner left forearm is common to that region. It appears to have only been recently completed.'

'I thought you may have been a magician.'

'There is no such thing as magic,' Mr Doyle said.

Kip frowned slightly. 'There is magic,' he said. 'I have seen it.'

'Really? Where?'

'On my island. There was a woman who could make bad spell on someone. Then they die.'

'Interesting. I would like to hear more later.'

Bradstreet took them to their cabins on the deck below. They were small, but made more comfortable with en-suite bathrooms. Jack and Mr Doyle were sharing while Phoebe and Scarlet were across the hall.

A whistle came from the main deck to announce the airship's departure. Jack went up to watch the ship cast off. The fog had cleared and airships were heading away in all directions. As the *Explorer* flew from Plymouth Harbour, Jack looked back at the coast. This adventure had to be a success. Gloria's life depended on it.

CHAPTER SEVENTEEN

At first glance, their room was exactly as they had left it, but Mr Doyle's keen eyes soon spotted a note on his bed.

'Ah ha,' he said. 'This is very encouraging.'

Jack read the note. 'It says, *Your lives are in danger. Turn back while you still can*. Mr Doyle, you have a strange idea of what is encouraging.'

'It means we're making progress,' Mr Doyle said. 'This is the same handwriting as the note Amelia received and the one about the British Museum.'

'How does this relate to Phillip?'

'I still don't know. We started investigating the reappearance of a watch and now we're on a hunt to find New Atlantis.'

'Maybe the robbery at the museum was a coincidence.'

'It would be an enormous coincidence.' Mr Doyle shook his head. 'No, I believe it is connected, but we don't have all the pieces yet.'

That night they ate dinner with Phoebe, Scarlet, Charles Spaulding and his men. Their meal was prepared by Sandra Clegg, the ship's elderly cook.

'That was lovely,' Mr Doyle said.

'I'm glad you enjoyed it, sir. Steak and kidney pie is one of my specialties.'

Mr Doyle asked Spaulding about his previous adventures.

'I've been to every continent except Antarctica,' he said. 'Mind you, some I've only passed through. White men have barely explored Africa or South America.'

'It's incredible that we haven't fully explored our own world,' Scarlet said. 'Yet we've reached into space with the metrotowers and they're even talking about sending a ship to the moon.'

'After the war, the League of Nations created treaties to protect native peoples,' Mr Spaulding said. 'And a good thing too, otherwise they would have been ruthlessly exploited by colonial powers.'

Mr Doyle turned to Kip and Tan. 'And what about you? Where have you travelled?'

Kip recounted their extensive expeditions through the South Pacific. Tan had lived in England for a time, but found it too cold.

'People should not live with white rain,' he said.

'You mean snow?'

'Snow is bad. Too cold.'

Mr Doyle turned to Kip. 'You said earlier about magic,' he said. 'Can you tell me more?'

Kip's eyes shifted. 'Should not speak of such things. Bad luck.'

'Surely not. You mentioned a woman.'

'She was a witch,' Kip said. 'Powerful woman.'

'A witch!' Jack cried. 'You mean with a broom and a—'

'Probably not that kind of witch,' Mr Doyle said gently.

'She lived alone,' Kip continued. 'Made medicine for people when they were ill, but she wanted payment.'

'And if someone did not pay?'

The man's face darkened. 'My friend had no money. She cursed him. She took a chicken bone and pointed it in his face and told him he would die.'

'And what happened?' Jack asked.

Kip shrugged. 'He died.'

Jack had heard about people dying from chicken bones before, but usually when they got stuck in their throats.

'There is no such thing as magic,' Mr Doyle said as Jack and Scarlet took a stroll with him around the deck the next morning. 'But the mind is a very powerful tool. An individual can lose the will to live.'

'Have you come across such a thing before?' Scarlet asked.

Mr Doyle sighed. 'I didn't want to live after Phillip's death,' he said. 'I went through a bad patch on my return to England.'

'I'm sorry to hear that, sir,' Jack said. 'It must have been very hard for you.'

'I was shell shocked from the war and I spent time in a soldier's hospital. Arriving home, I tried speaking to Amelia, but she blamed me for Phillip's death. I sank into a despair that lasted months.'

Jack found it hard to believe that such an exuberant man as Mr Doyle could be affected by such unhappiness.

'What finally brought you out of it?' Scarlet asked. 'How did you—'

'Come back to life? A woman approached me because her brother had been murdered. After hearing her story, I realised her life was also in danger. I tracked down the killer and was able to stop a further tragedy.'

'So helping someone else also helped you.'

'Precisely. I often think we do not exist for ourselves, but for each other.' Tears pricked the corners of Mr Doyle's eyes. 'The woman I helped was Gloria.'

No-one said anything for a moment. Jack knew Gloria was more than a receptionist to Mr Doyle. She cared for him like a mother. Now Jack began to appreciate how much Gloria must mean to him. Her presence had literally saved his life.

Phoebe arrived, dressed again in her trousers and a shirt. Jack wasn't sure he would ever get used to it.

'We're due to arrive in Morocco soon,' she said.

'The Captain intends to stock up on our supplies.'

'Hasn't he already done that?' Mr Doyle said. 'The hold seems full.'

'It's just a precaution. We don't know how long we'll be away.'

Jack could tell that Mr Doyle was keen to keep moving. Every moment wasted meant that Gloria and Professor Clarke's condition would continue to deteriorate.

'And we have an additional mystery,' Phoebe went on. 'It seems there is a thief on board. Last night Sandra, the cook, discovered food missing. She saw someone running away down the passageway. She gave chase, but they escaped.'

'Interesting,' Mr Doyle said. 'We will investigate. It will keep our mental muscles limber.'

Mr Doyle thanked Phoebe, and they all went to find Sandra in the kitchen preparing vegetables.

'He was small,' Sandra told them, describing the thief. 'It was very dark so I didn't get a good look at him. He was headed towards the stern.'

Mr Doyle nodded thoughtfully. 'Have you worked for Mr Bradstreet long?'

'This is my first voyage,' the woman said. 'But I've been a cook for several years.'

They approached Tobias Bradstreet next, who confessed to being equally puzzled by the incident. Most of the crew had worked for him for years. They had no reason to steal food: the rations were generous.

'All this reminds me of a Brinkie Buckeridge story,' Scarlet said when they returned to Mr Doyle and Jack's cabin.

'Doesn't everything?' Jack asked.

She glared at him. 'Brinkie's adventures are so true to life it's inevitable we should come across similar situations ourselves. Anyway, Brinkie was on a ship heading to Brazil to visit a cousin.'

'The cannibal cousin?'

'No. Another cousin. Abernathy.'

'This one has never eaten human flesh?'

'What's this fixation you have with cannibalism?'

'I'm just checking.'

'Food was being stolen on board the ship. The captain was ruthless, making his crew walk the plank as he tried to determine the identity of the secret eater. Finally there remained only the captain and Abernathy.'

'Bazookas.'

'You'll never guess who it turned out to be,' Scarlet said smugly.

'Allow me,' Mr Doyle intervened. 'There was a stowaway.'

Scarlet looked at him in amazement. 'Have you read the book?' she asked. 'I know you're a purveyor of fine literature.'

'I haven't read that particular volume, but it seemed likely that once all the other possibilities were eliminated—the other crew members, that is—then what remained was most likely.'

Mr Doyle removed an odd-looking rock from his pocket and, dusting it off, decided it was a lump of cheese. Popping it into his mouth, he said, 'We must remain alert. A stowaway could damage the engines, or the balloon, or some other vital piece of equipment. They could even bring about the destruction of this airship.'

CHAPTER EIGHTEEN

A few days later they reached Rabat, a city on the coast of Morocco. Much of the trade conducted on the continent passed through here on its way to Europe. Mr Doyle decided to stay aboard the *Explorer*, so Phoebe offered to take Jack and Scarlet around the city while the airship was restocked.

The sea was a blanket of sparkling diamonds and the air warm, filled with competing scents of curries, spices and flavoured tobacco. The streets were narrow and Phoebe was careful to keep away from dark alleys. Jack was nervous about wandering around the foreign city—it felt like visiting another planet—but fear soon turned to fascination. Most buildings were constructed from adobe, painted blue and ivory. Others were stone.

One of the most interesting parts of the city was the Hassan Tower, an enormous square edifice dominating the landscape and surrounded by hundreds of columns.

Phoebe briefly explained its history. 'The tower is the minaret of a mosque. Construction began in the twelfth century, but it was never finished.' She pointed at the columns. 'They were also part of the mosque. It would have been one of the wonders of the world, if completed.'

'I had no idea anything like this existed,' Jack said.

'Europeans often forget the accomplishments of cultures different to our own.'

Late in the day, they wandered through the market. Awnings of crimson, yellow and blue hung over the alleys, protecting the streets from the hot afternoon sun. The clamour was overwhelming, disconcerting—and intoxicating. Hundreds of stallholders, many with wares Jack had never seen, tried to catch the attention of visitors. They sold water pipes for smoking, herbs, brightly coloured fabrics, jewellery and religious paraphernalia. Stallholders cooked food on hotplates over small fires, filling the air with the smells of curry, turmeric and chilli.

They spotted a familiar face among the crowd.

'There's Reg Smythe,' Jack said.

'Hello passengers,' he said, smiling as they pushed through the bustle. 'You've been allowed out for the day.'

'As have you,' Phoebe said.

'Please join me for coffee.'

They followed Smythe into a tiny café adjoining the marketplace and found a table at a window where they could watch the passing traffic. Men sat about, smoking from water pipes, the smell of aromatic tobacco filling the air.

Smythe ordered coffee for himself and Phoebe, and hot chocolates for Jack and Scarlet.

When their drinks arrived, Jack took a cautious sip. His eyes popped. *It tasted heavenly.*

'You must tell us about your previous adventures,' Phoebe said to Smythe.

He waved a hand. 'There's little to tell,' he said. 'And none of it would compare to your own. You've been to Egypt, I understand.'

Phoebe spoke about her experiences. 'Camels are a wonderful form of transport,' she said, 'but they take some getting used to.'

'In what way?' Jack asked.

'You need to sit back when the camel stands up or sits down. The first time I climbed onto one, I fell off and landed on my head!'

'The pyramids and the Sphinx must be quite incredible,' Smythe said.

Phoebe nodded. 'There has been quite a bit of conjecture about how they were built. Scientists believe ancient people were quite advanced when it came to engineering. Others suggest more outrageous theories.'

'Such as?'

'Oh, visitors from other worlds.'

'What?' Jack said, astonished.

Reg Smythe sat up. 'I've seen many ancient temples,' he said. 'You *do* wonder how they built them using such old techniques.'

'Which ones have you seen?' Phoebe asked.

Smythe laughed. 'Too many to list.' He glanced at his watch. 'I'd better keep moving. I promised the captain I'd pick up a few supplies.' He paid for their drinks and headed off.

'I suppose we'd better do the same,' Phoebe said. 'I promised Ignatius I'd buy him some cheese.'

On the way to a cheese merchant in the middle of the market, they stopped to watch a snake charmer who had members of the crowd transfixed as a cobra moved about hypnotically on a mat.

'Your friend, Mr Beethoven, would enjoy this,' Jack said to Scarlet. 'It sounds like his music.'

'His music is *nothing* like this,' Scarlet said. 'And you must develop an appreciation for the finer arts.'

'I do like music,' Jack said. 'Just not classical.'

Phoebe completed her purchase. 'There's a new style of music called jazz that's becoming very popular in the United States,' she said, smiling at Jack. 'It has a beat you can tap your foot to and songs you can sing.'

'I'll keep an eye, er, ear out for it.'

They eventually made their way back to the *Explorer*.

'I've kept tabs on Ignatius over the years,' Phoebe said to them. 'I've been most impressed by his career.'

'You've never been married?' Jack asked.

'Jack! Are you proposing?'

Jack turned so red that Scarlet almost fell over laughing.

The archaeologist continued more seriously. 'No,' she said. 'My only near-miss was with Ignatius. My whole life has been one of exploration. I've never had time for families. I would have loved to have children, but there was always too much to do. Besides,' she added. 'You never forget your first love.'

When night fell the great engines of the *Explorer* roared back to life. Smoke billowed from the rear of the vessel as the airship left the coast behind.

Jack and Scarlet went out onto the deck to watch Rabat shrink into the distance.

'It must be fantastic,' Jack said. 'To spend your life exploring new places.'

'What do you think will happen to Mr Doyle when all this is over?' Scarlet asked.

'What do you mean?'

'It's just that he and Phoebe seem to be getting on very well.'

'They are old friends,' Jack said, staring at Scarlet. 'What are you trying to say?'

'I'm saying they seem to be getting along *really* well.'

'Have you been eating too much beef jerky? Are you saying they might get married?'

'Stranger things have happened.'

Jack returned with Scarlet to his cabin to find Mr Doyle lying across the bed, hands behind his head, staring thoughtfully at the ceiling. More food had been found missing from the kitchen, he told them. He had made up his mind to nab the thief that night.

'How will you do that?' Scarlet asked.

'I intend to use a very large mousetrap,' Mr Doyle said. 'To which I will attach a massive piece of cheese. When they attempt to take the food, a huge arm will fly down, pinning them helplessly to the floor.'

Jack and Scarlet stared at him.

'Just a little joke,' he said. 'I assume you're familiar with the story of Hansel and Gretel?'

'The kids in the forest?' Jack said.

'And the witch and breadcrumbs,' Scarlet added.

'There is much to be learnt from children's stories.'

With that enigmatic comment, the detective said no more.

Eating dinner with Phoebe and the others in the galley, Jack found himself peering more closely at the motley group. There were many he had not met. Could one of them be the thief? Or was there really a stowaway?

After the meal, Scarlet joined Jack and Mr Doyle in their cabin. The detective planned to hunt down the thief in the dead of night. Phoebe was invited too, but declined, with her usual dry wit, saying she was busy doing her nails. Jack and Scarlet settled into armchairs to sleep for a few hours. When Jack awoke next, the detective had made them all hot chocolate.

'Come, you two,' Mr Doyle said. 'It's time to follow the breadcrumbs.'

Breadcrumbs?

'If you say so,' Jack said.

Mr Doyle lit a kerosene lamp and they followed him to the galley where they found the door ajar. In the kitchen, the pantry door was also open.

'Good,' the detective said. 'Our visitor has taken the bait.'

'I must confess to being a little lost,' Scarlet said.

'Surely you remember the fairytale?' Mr Doyle said. 'A trail of breadcrumbs led the children back to safety after they fell into the clutches of the evil witch.' He waved the lamp over the floor, revealing a crystalline substance glittering in the pale light. 'We're using sugar.'

'How—'

'I arranged with Sandra to leave a box of goods outside the kitchen. A tear in the box is leaving a trail.'

They followed the glimmering path down several flights of stairs. They passed a crewman who glanced at them curiously. Mr Doyle gave him a friendly smile without speaking. After several minutes they reached a door at the top of a metal staircase leading into the cargo hold, a gloomy room filled with boxes of supplies, a steam-powered submarine and something that looked like a tank.

'It appears Mr Bradstreet is well equipped.'

They headed towards a pile of boxes in a corner. Mr Doyle waved the lantern about, making the shadows dance and dive like ghosts.

'Please show yourself,' he called. 'We mean you no harm.'

Silence.

'If you do not show yourself,' Mr Doyle continued, 'I will be forced to call the captain, who will confine you to the brig. I understand it is full of cockroaches.' He paused. 'And spiders.'

One of the shadows broke away and a girl emerged into the dull light. Pushing back her long hair, she revealed a dirty face, small eyes and broad lips. She was about fifteen.

Blimey, thought Jack.

'Who are you?' she demanded. 'You have no right to ask me questions!' Despite her appearance, she was well spoken.

'I believe we have every right,' Mr Doyle responded. 'Can you tell us why you're here?'

The girl glared at them defiantly.

'I believe I can guess.' Mr Doyle turned to Jack and Scarlet. 'Does this young lady remind you of anyone?'

Jack started to shake his head. Then he looked a little harder at the girl, who simply glared back. Under the dirt, her face was actually quite pretty. And something about her eyes...

'Professor Clarke!' he said.

'He's my grandfather!' The girl clenched her fists, as if ready to attack them with her bare hands. 'You're responsible for putting him in hospital!'

'We did no such thing,' Mr Doyle said. He introduced everyone. 'We are involved in an investigation to discover what happened to your grandfather—and why.'

'You're lying,' the girl cried. 'You're going to be sorry for what you've done! He's in a coma...and...and...'

She looked ready to burst into tears.

'Mr Doyle is telling the truth,' Scarlet said gently. 'We *are* trying to find a cure for your grandfather as well as a friend of ours who was also attacked.'

She explained the chain of events, leaving out the details about Mr Doyle's son.

'Come with us,' Scarlet said, 'and we'll explain everything.'

The girl's face was smeared with dirty tears. 'You want to put me in jail,' she said. 'Or throw me off the ship.'

'We could have half the crew down here in minutes if we wanted to arrest you,' Mr Doyle said. 'But I think it's illegal to throw people off airships.'

The girl sighed, sagging against the stack of boxes. 'I'll come with you,' she said, 'but you'd better not try anything.'

'What's your name?' Jack asked.

'Clarice,' she said, taking another step forward. 'Clarice Clarke.'

They took her back to Phoebe and Scarlet's cabin. Clarice's attitude changed completely when she was introduced to Phoebe. 'My grandfather speaks of you all the time,' she gushed. 'He says you're the bee's knees!'

'Thank you, my dear,' Phoebe said. 'I've followed your grandfather's work for years. His articles on the Greek–Roman traces of the Atlantis legend are the best in the field. But how did you end up on board the *Explorer*?'

Clarice explained that she had travelled to London after learning about the attack on her grandfather. While visiting him in hospital, she saw Mr Doyle and his team. Staking out their apartment, she came to the erroneous conclusion that they were involved in attacking her grandfather.

'Why was he attacked?' Clarice asked, looking ready to burst into tears again. 'Why did they hurt him?'

Jack felt his heart melting. Clarice had been through so much over the past few days. Trailing them to the airship was incredible enough, but stowing aboard without being discovered was nothing short of a miracle.

'We don't know who harmed your grandfather,' Mr Doyle said, grimly. 'But I promise you: we will find out.'

CHAPTER NINETEEN

Phoebe settled Clarice in a spare cot in her room before rejoining Mr Doyle and the others. 'She's sound asleep,' she said. 'I don't think she's had a good night's rest in weeks. Understandable, considering the circumstances.'

It turned out Clarice had been orphaned and taken in by her grandfather at a young age. Jack understood this pain: losing his own parents was the most traumatic experience he had ever endured.

The next morning the captain began their final course corrections to Smollett's Island. Mr Doyle broke the news to Tobias Bradstreet about the stowaway.

He was less than pleased. 'I run a tight operation,'

he said. 'She should be thrown into the brig for the duration of the voyage.'

But he calmed down when Mr Doyle explained the girl's reasons for stowing away.

'Just make certain she stays out of trouble. This is a historic expedition. I don't want it ruined by the actions of a silly girl.'

The *Explorer* cut across the ocean like a bird the next morning as Jack and Scarlet strolled the decks with Clarice. She and her grandfather had travelled all over the world together, and she had learnt a great deal about ancient history and archaeology.

'I don't know what I'll do if I lost him,' she said, staring out at the clouds. 'I can't imagine life alone.'

'Don't you have any other family?' Jack asked.

'I've got an aunt, but I haven't seen her for years.'

'Best not to worry about things before they happen,' Scarlet said. 'We'll find a cure with Phoebe and Mr Doyle's help.'

Jack pointed to the far horizon. 'What's that out there?' he asked. 'Is that an island?'

'I think it is,' Scarlet said. 'Let's tell Mr Doyle.'

They found the detective. 'I believe you're right,' he said. 'Which means that now is probably a good time to have a word with the captain.'

'What about?' Jack asked.

But Mr Doyle did not speak again until they reached the bridge. Here they found the ship's officers deep in discussion with Tobias Bradstreet.

'Are we interrupting?' Mr Doyle asked.

'Somewhat,' said Captain Malone rudely.

'Is there a problem?'

'We think so,' Bradstreet said. 'There is an airship following us.'

'Are you sure?'

'There's no reason for it to be out here. We're completely off the normal shipping lanes.'

'Oh dear,' Mr Doyle said. 'Perhaps I should have spoken up earlier.'

'About what?' Tobias Bradstreet looked baffled. 'What are you talking about?'

Mr Doyle pointed at the first officer, Reg Smythe, who was examining a navigation map. 'I suggest you place Mr Smythe under guard,' he said. 'He is a danger to this ship.'

'What?' Smythe's mouth fell open. 'That's outrageous! I don't know what you're talking about!'

Mr Doyle said to Bradstreet, 'I hope you don't mind, but I made a point of reading Mr Smythe's curriculum vitae.'

'You broke into my office?'

'All for a good cause. Mr Smythe's employment history states that he was born in Surrey, attending St John's School for Boys before joining the Royal Air Force and serving with distinction during the war. At its conclusion, he worked in the merchant air navy, transporting goods across India for three years before returning to England.'

Smythe was furious. 'What of it?' he demanded.

'It is all a lie,' said Mr Doyle.

'How dare you! I'm a man of my word!'

'Poppycock. You were born and raised in Newcastle. Your father was a farrier and you went on to follow in his footsteps. When the war began, you rose no higher than the rank of able seaman aboard a navy ship.'

'That's…that's…'

'You supposedly spent time in Nepal,' Mr Doyle continued. 'Yet had no idea what I meant when I mentioned the Goddess of the Earth.'

'I—'

'What does it mean? Quickly, man!'

'I…I refuse—'

'You mean you can't. It is the translation for the word *Chomolungma*, the local Nepalese name for Everest, as anyone who has ever lived or worked in that region knows. In addition, your training in the operations of an airship began less than six months ago. You—'

Reg Smythe produced a gun and waved it at them. 'You're some sort of demon,' he snarled. 'But that will not affect our plans. You were all doomed anyway.' He pointed the gun at Captain Malone. 'I might start with our stout captain.'

A shot rang out—but the captain did not fall. The gun flew from Smythe's hand and cluttered to one side. He doubled over, grasping his bloody hand. He made another grab for the weapon, but the crew had him helpless on the ground in seconds.

Jack turned in amazement to see Mr Doyle's coat pocket now had a hole in it. The detective pulled out his hand to reveal his gun, Clarabelle, a trail of smoke still curling from the barrel.

'I dislike shooting people,' Mr Doyle said. 'Even a scoundrel as wretched as Smythe.'

The first officer was handcuffed and dragged off to the brig. Tobias Bradstreet was remarkably composed, but Captain Malone's face was white. Jack helped him to a nearby chair.

'Ignatius!' Bradstreet said. 'How on earth did you know he was a fraud?'

'Just a simple assemblage of the clues,' Mr Doyle said. 'His ignorance about Everest was just the beginning. Once I checked his resumé I discovered several other glaring inconsistencies.

'Although he had travelled, I could tell his native accent was from the north of England, not the south. I noticed him bend over the other day, but his stance made it obvious he had worked with horses. Farriers have a particular way of holding the horses' legs and he did that instinctively.'

Jack spoke up. 'But how did you know he had been in the navy?'

'Simplicity itself. Navy men have a distinctive manner of walking. It is a rolling gait. With airship pilots it is quite different. As to his training, I only had to observe him using the controls for a few minutes to ascertain he was an amateur.'

Captain Malone mopped sweat from his face. 'I just thought he was out of practice,' he admitted.

'More than that, unfortunately. He was a complete fraud.'

One of the crew approached the captain. 'Sir? That other airship's gaining on us.'

Captain Malone grabbed a pair of binoculars. 'It *is* gaining,' he said. 'But we'll reach Smollett's Island first.'

Bradstreet pointed to a mountain range dominating the island. 'Can you navigate us past that peak so we'll be out of sight? You can drop us off and continue on. There's an island chain west of here. They may believe you're heading for them and follow you there instead.'

The captain started yelling orders. The engines surged and the *Explorer* crossed the coast, rounded the mountains and rapidly descended.

'This is not the expedition I had in mind,' Bradstreet said. 'There are emergency packs in the aft cargo bay near the exit. Grab one each and make ready to disembark.'

Bradstreet said he would join them shortly. He asked Mr Doyle to locate Charles Spaulding, his men, and all the women on board. The latter he wanted evacuated in case things turned nasty.

The group assembled in the cargo bay. Spaulding and his men prepared their equipment. Mr Doyle checked his pockets, taking out a piece of cheese and gnawing it, deep in thought.

Suddenly the *Explorer* dropped. Scarlet looked worried as they peered through an observation portal to see the landscape fly past. Jack's stomach filled with butterflies when they swooped in low over a beach.

'Don't be nervous,' Jack said to Phoebe. 'Everything will be fine.'

'Who's nervous?' she asked, breaking into a grin. 'We might be walking the streets of New Atlantis in the next few hours.'

'Or shot out of the sky before we make land,' Scarlet muttered.

A pair of crewmen readied the lower doors as the *Explorer*'s steam engines went into reverse. The vessel shuddered to an untidy halt and Spaulding dispensed backpacks. He, Kip and Tan all carried rifles.

The doors opened, revealing a sandy beach. The men dropped a chain-metal ladder to the ground.

Mr Bradstreet joined them. They scrambled down, assembling in the shadow beneath the airship. Jack peered up at the ship's enormous underbelly, hovering like a thundercloud.

He felt dazed. After spending days on board the *Explorer*, they were now on a deserted tropical beach in the middle of nowhere.

The airship's engines roared to full power and the *Explorer* moved on, following the beach as it curved around to a distant headland. It would be far out at sea within minutes. Jack's eyes followed the ship longingly. He wondered when they would see it again.

The sun beat down. It was almost lunchtime and Jack's stomach was rumbling.

'I hope this works,' Bradstreet said. 'With any luck, they won't realise we're on the island and they'll continue following the *Explorer*.'

'We should take refuge in the jungle,' Mr Spaulding said. 'We're sitting ducks out here.'

The group pushed through a thick tangle of undergrowth into a small clearing. Palm trees created a canopy. Ferns choked the ground, while vines spanned the jungle like rigging on a sailing ship. Mostly it was a sea of green, but there were splashes of colour: orchids, lilies, violets, protea. Jack had never seen anything like it before.

'Where to now?' Mr Doyle asked.

Tobias Bradstreet turned to Phoebe. 'What would you advise? Was the Broken Sun specific as to where to search?'

'No, but I have an idea.' She pointed at two nearby mountain peaks that dominated the skyline. 'Plato said that the original city lay beyond the pillars of Hercules.'

'That's generally regarded as being a reference to the Strait of Gibraltar,' Bradstreet said.

Phoebe nodded. 'But I wonder if the Atlanteans may have adopted a similar plan for New Atlantis, a location where two mountain tops act as a gate?'

Bradstreet sighed. 'I don't have a better idea. At least from up there we'll be able to see most of the island.'

'And something may stand out.'

They continued into the forest. It quickly became apparent that Bradstreet had chosen well when he employed Charles Spaulding and his men: they wielded machetes as if born with them in their hands. Despite the thick terrain, they made it yield, carving a path for the rest to follow.

There had been a light breeze on the beach, but the jungle was hot and sticky. Jack was sweating beneath his coat, and his pack was heavy with supplies.

Wild birds gave strange cries. A flock of red-and-green parrots broke from some trees and disappeared into the distance. The scream of a strange creature cut the air, and Jack caught a glimpse of fur as it scampered away on faraway branches.

An explosion sounded behind them.

'Good Lord!' Bradstreet cried.

'That sounds like cannon fire,' Mr Doyle said.

'We need to go back.'

'I wouldn't advise it,' Spaulding said. 'We should make headway while we can.'

'The *Explorer* is *my* ship,' Bradstreet said, 'and her crew my responsibility.'

They raced back along the makeshift path to the beach. The *Explorer* was now off the coast, heading west. Another vessel, a black cigar-shaped airship with a silver gondola, was directly behind. A brass cannon protruded from it. Mr Doyle produced his goggles to take a closer look.

Boom!

'They're firing on our ship!' Bradstreet said. 'That's outrageous!'

'It looks like things are about to become a great deal worse,' Mr Spaulding said grimly.

A light, brighter than the sun, appeared on one side of the *Explorer's* balloon. Then the entire hydrogen-filled cell erupted into a ball of flame.

Ka-boom!

Everyone screamed as the *Explorer* tumbled from the sky. Trailing smoke, it disappeared beyond a range of far hills, crashing into the water.

'Those monsters,' Phoebe cried. 'All those people on the ship...'

'Could the crew have survived?' Mr Doyle asked.

'There is some hope,' Bradstreet said, looking ill. 'The *Explorer* is designed to float, but I don't know if the ship—or the people aboard—could survive such an impact.'

'More problems coming,' Kip said.

Tan had lifted his arm towards the distant hills. The black vessel had turned and was now heading in their direction.

CHAPTER TWENTY

'They're only a few minutes away,' Mr Doyle said. 'We need to get off this beach. We're too exposed.'

Charles Spaulding stroked his chin, formulating an idea. 'We've already marked a path here. I suggest we continue back to the mountains, but first go further down the beach to locate a natural entrance.'

'And leave this as a ruse?' Mr Doyle said.

'Indeed.'

Any pursuer would see the trail hacked into the jungle and follow it. They would eventually realise they had been fooled, but it would at least buy the group some time.

'I will cover tracks,' Kip suggested. 'Give us head start.'

The expedition headed down the beach with Kip using a branch to smooth over the sand behind them. A natural glade opened into the jungle. Carefully navigating the vegetation, they continued inland with Charles Spaulding and Kip in the lead.

Within an hour they were far from the coast and nearing the two mountain tops. Jack fell into step with Clarice. 'I wonder who's in charge of that airship,' he said.

'Probably the people who tried to kill my grandfather and your friend.' The girl didn't say anything for a moment. 'Do you think we're really going to find a cure?'

'Mr Doyle can do it if anyone can.'

'How long have you known him?'

Jack explained how he had come to be with Mr Doyle after the deaths of his parents. 'He's been training us to become detectives.'

'Both of you? Scarlet too?'

'Yes.'

Scarlet was walking ahead of them. 'You think that a strange idea?' she asked.

'Not at all. My grandfather says that equal rights for women is long overdue.'

The girls went on to have an animated conversation about the women's movement. Both of them, it turned out, admired Emmeline Pankhurst, the famous suffragette. The discussion shifted to their current predicament. Jack voiced the opinion that Mr Doyle would apprehend the evildoers.

'Is he really that good?'

Clarice was enthralled as Jack and Scarlet described some of their adventures. The more Jack spoke to the girl, the more he liked her.

'Still, this is a different environment,' she said. 'This isn't England.'

'No,' Jack had to agree, glancing about at the native jungle. He wiped sweat from his face. 'It isn't!'

'My grandfather and I have been through some tough scrapes over the years,' Clarice said. 'A sinking ship. Lost in the Yukon for a week. We were even held hostage by cannibals.'

'Cannibals?' Scarlet's eyes lit up.

'Don't get her started,' Jack implored.

'We've been through a lot.' Tears shone in Clarice's eyes. 'I don't know what I'd do without him.'

Scarlet squeezed her hand. 'Mr Doyle will get to the bottom of this.'

'I hope so.' Clarice's eyes narrowed. 'I hate the man who did this. He deserves to pay for what he's done.'

Jack and Scarlet exchanged glances. *Who is she talking about?*

'You mean whoever hurt your grandfather?' Jack said.

Scarlet stopped her. 'You know who's behind this, don't you?'

'No, not at all,' Clarice said, but she was blushing.

Scarlet called Mr Doyle over and he quizzed the girl. 'You had best tell us what you know,' he said. 'Two heads are better than one. And four heads are better than three, but not nearly as good as... Well, you know what I mean.'

Clarice sighed. 'There was a man who came to visit my grandfather several months ago,' she admitted. 'His name was George Darrow, a Darwinist doctor. He was asking lots of questions about Atlantis and about something called the Living Machine. He became very angry when Grandfather refused to answer him, and stormed out.'

'We should speak to the others about this,' Mr Doyle said. 'They may have something to offer.'

He called a short break. As they sipped from their water flasks, Clarice told her tale to the group. Tobias Bradstreet shook his head, saying he had never heard of Darrow or the Living Machine, but Phoebe was nodding.

'I first heard of Darrow years ago,' she said. 'Like many people, he wanted to know about Atlantis, but he had one specific interest—the Living Machine. It's supposed to be an invention of the Atlanteans. Apparently it was an interface that could join the thoughts of a man with a machine.'

'How could such a thing be possible?' Bradstreet said.

'It sounds unlikely, I know, but there may be something to it. I heard a rumour some years ago that a fossil had been discovered in a dig in Cairo. Half animal, half machine.'

Charles Spaulding spoke up. 'This is all very interesting, but I suggest we keep moving. Those people may be close behind.' He looked around. 'Wait a minute. We're missing someone.'

'Sandra Clegg,' Bradstreet said.

She was nowhere to be seen. Fanning out, they conducted a quick search.

'When did anyone last see her?' Charles Spaulding asked.

Phoebe recalled her on the beach when they saw the airship.

'I hope she's all right,' Scarlet said. 'Maybe she's lost.'

'Or had an accident,' Clarice said.

'There may be quite a different explanation,' Mr Doyle mused. 'She may have purposefully separated from our group.'

'But why?' Bradstreet asked.

'She told us this was her first journey aboard the *Explorer*,' Mr Doyle said. 'Did she have references?'

'She did.' The man thought for a moment. 'But I didn't need to contact her previous employers: during the interview, it became clear that she knew how to run a kitchen.'

'Sandra Clegg—if that is her real name—certainly had experience,' Mr Doyle said. 'But she may have been planted aboard ship, like Reg Smythe, to infiltrate our operation.'

'What will we do?' Scarlet asked.

'We need to keep moving,' Phoebe said. 'The people who shot down the *Explorer* might be right behind us.'

'But she may just be lost,' Mr Spaulding said. 'I'll

go back with Kip and see if we can locate her.'

When they returned half an hour later, Mr Spaulding had a piece of torn fabric in his hand.

'That's part of Sandra's apron,' Bradstreet said. 'And is that…?'

'Blood?' Mr Spaulding said. 'It is. We found this some distance down the trail near a ravine. I tried calling down into the gorge, but there was no reply.'

'And no other trace of her?' Mr Doyle asked.

'None.'

'Then we must move on.'

'No!' Bradstreet said. 'We must go back and search.'

'I understand your feelings,' Mr Doyle said, 'but she may not wish to be found. And if Mr Spaulding and his men have not been able to find her, then it's unlikely we could.'

'It was a very deep ravine,' Spaulding explained. 'No-one could have survived a fall to the bottom.'

Bradstreet sighed. 'I suppose you're right.'

Spaulding peered up the slope. 'It looks like a ridge runs between the two mountains,' he said. 'We'll be able to see most of the island from there.'

'Good thinking,' Bradstreet said. 'Let's get moving.'

They continued uphill. Jack wondered about Sandra Clegg. Had she been taken by a wild animal? Or was she in league with the people in the black airship? She could have signalled to them—possibly with a mirror—meaning their pursuers might be close behind.

At the top of the ridge, an ancient crater covered in

waist-high grass, was nestled between the mountains. The sides were steep with a few ravines. A stream tumbled over a ledge of the nearest peak, falling hundreds of feet into a pool below.

'How does the water get up there?' Jack asked. 'It's going uphill.'

'It must be an underground spring,' Mr Spaulding said. 'Forcing its way through the rock until it finds a gap.'

'Looks strange,' Kip agreed.

From here they could see much of the island to the north. The black airship had disappeared. Jack wasn't sure if he felt relieved or worried.

As to the *Explorer*, there was still no sign.

They continued along the ridge until a distant thud came from the jungle behind them. It sounded like the felling of a tree. Wordlessly, they all stopped and gazed down the slope. Another crash reverberated through the undergrowth.

'What on earth is it?' Phoebe asked.

'I have no idea,' Charles Spaulding said. 'I've never seen anything move through the jungle like that.'

They watched the thick foliage as something—or two somethings—moved through the undergrowth, shaking the canopy above them. Whatever they were, they were travelling at an incredible pace.

Finally the rustling mass reached the steep slope of the mountain where the jungle thinned, and two enormous figures appeared. They looked like knights of old, but they were machines in the shape of men, steam firing from a dozen joints. Cogs, gears and pistons shone in the afternoon light.

'What are they?' Bradstreet hissed. 'Some sort of robot?'

Spaulding produced a pair of binoculars. 'Those aren't machines. Not entirely.'

'Is it a kind of battle suit?' Mr Doyle asked.

'I think so. I think I can see faces behind the helmets.' Spaulding lowered his binoculars. 'Whatever they are, they're coming straight towards us.'

CHAPTER TWENTY-ONE

The machine men moved with terrifying speed. While it had taken Jack and the others more than an hour to climb the slope, their pursuers would reach the crater in minutes.

'To that ravine!' Spaulding shouted.

They scrambled down the crater's edge and raced through the long grass. Jack arrowed towards the ravine with Scarlet close behind.

'Jack!' Scarlet yelled. 'We're going the wrong way!'

He skidded to a halt. *Bazookas*, he thought. *Scarlet's right.* The others were racing towards a different ravine. He and Scarlet were running in the opposite direction. It was too late to do anything about it now. Their pursuers would be over the rise in seconds.

He looked back to the ravine—and had an awful realisation. 'It doesn't lead anywhere,' he said in dismay. 'It's a dead end.'

The stream, spilling from the peak he had seen earlier, ended in a spectacular waterfall at the bottom before trickling into a deep pool. Darkness lay behind the waterfall.

Jack grabbed Scarlet's arm. 'That way!' he said. 'I think we can take cover.'

Reaching the cascade, Jack looked over his shoulder just as the machine men appeared at the edge of the crater. He'd never seen anything like them. Their engines were worn like backpacks. The power fed through copper pipes and tubes to servos built into their knees, ankles, elbows and wrists. Helmets with slots for their eyes enclosed their heads. Retractable guns had been built into their forearms. Their hands were three times normal size.

The machine men had not spotted them. The recess behind the waterfall was small, but looked like it could accommodate two people.

'Take my hand,' Jack told Scarlet.

They stepped through the shower. The roar of the water was like an avalanche. Jack almost slipped on the mossy stones as his eyes searched the gloom. The recess was larger than he had first thought, and a crack in the rock led to a dry enclosure.

The torrent was not as loud back here. Jack could

still see glimpses of the grassy plain, but much of it was shielded by the veil of water.

Scarlet tugged at his arm. 'I think they're coming this way,' she said. 'Let's go back further.'

She was right. Two huge shapes, distorted by the water screen, were moving towards them. They slipped further into the gloom. It was a tight squeeze and Jack found himself face to face with Scarlet, shoved so hard against her he could feel the beat of her heart. He felt himself blushing.

Thank God it's dark in here.

Her lips were only inches away. Water dripped from her red hair, down her face, and nestled in the crook of her chin before sliding down her throat. Her eyes shifted to his. She looked away. He could smell her breath. What had she eaten for breakfast? Honey on toast?

Crazy, he thought. *Crazy. Crazy. Crazy.*

But her breath was intoxicating. His heart was so loud that he was amazed the machine men could not hear it.

Thud...thud...thud...

Jack touched her arm and their eyes met again. She touched his shoulder...

...and the wall gave way.

Jack felt himself falling. He threw out an arm, but there was nothing to grab. He and Scarlet both cried out, crashing a few feet to a rocky floor.

Oof!

It was dark—wherever they were. But the wall hadn't

collapsed. They had, in fact, leaned against a stone door that had opened onto a small room. Jack caught a final glimpse of the waterfall beyond before the door swung shut, drowning them in darkness.

They groped at the stone entryway, searching for a handle, but the surface was completely smooth.

They were trapped.

Complete panic seized Jack. *No-one saw us come in here*, he thought. *Which means they'll never find us.* Searchers could look for days or weeks or months and never work out where they'd gone. They might even look behind the waterfall, but not find the secret door.

He started slapping the stonework, but then a light flickered on, banishing the darkness. Scarlet held a burning match.

'We're carrying backpacks,' she reminded him. 'Packed with supplies. Food and water. Matches. Candles.'

'Hmm.' In his panic, he had forgotten. 'Nice idea, that match.'

'Thanks.'

He rooted through his pack and produced a candle. Now with the aid of light, they continued searching for a lever or handle, but with no success.

'I don't think the others saw us head for the waterfall,' Scarlet said.

'They didn't.'

'Which means...'

'Yes,' he said. 'Cannibalism is on the menu.'

'Don't be silly.'

'Who's being silly?'

They examined the enclosure. It was square chamber about four feet across.

'This is man-made,' Scarlet said. 'Or woman-made. There was a Brinkie Buckeridge novel, *The Adventure of the Glass Warrior*, where an entire civilisation, made up only of women, survived for centuries in an underground cave.'

'Really? No men.'

'Not one.'

'So how did they…er, reproduce?'

'That's never explained.'

Jack turned his attention to their surroundings. Scarlet was right. No rocky cave could be this perfectly formed. Fine grooves on the walls indicated where the stone had been chiselled away.

Jack pressed against the back wall and it gave way, spinning around on a central pivot. He shone the candle into the gap. Stairs led down into the darkness.

'I think we should follow them,' he said.

'What about the others?' Scarlet asked.

'They may never find us here. We're better off seeing where this leads.'

The steps were smooth and the walls rough. The ceiling was too high for light from the flickering candle to penetrate. The passageway spiralled downwards, finally ending in a chamber covered in hieroglyphics.

'This looks very old,' Scarlet murmured. 'I think it's Ancient Sumerian.'

'Really? I thought it may have been Eskimoan. Maybe tenth-century BC.'

'Don't be silly.'

'Sorry, it comes so naturally. What makes you think it's Sumerian?'

Scarlet pointed. 'There's the symbol we saw on the Broken Sun for the number two,' she said. 'And a number seven over here.'

They *were* the same symbols. A story was being played out, the images showing a king and his subjects, surrounded by bushels of grain, chariots, vases and trees. Below them was a picture of two columns, waves and boats.

'I think this is the story of Atlantis,' Scarlet said. 'Describing how the city was destroyed and the people left by boat.'

'I'd probably find this more interesting if we weren't involved in a life and death struggle,' Jack said. His candle was shrinking dangerously. While they still had plenty of matches, they couldn't stay there forever. 'Let's try pushing on the wall. It might open like the others.'

But it didn't. They spent several minutes pushing and shoving from all directions, but it didn't budge. Panic was still nagging at the back of Jack's mind. He reached down into his pocket and touched the compass from his parents.

How do we get out of here? he asked. *There must be a way.*

If he was expecting an answer, he didn't get one. His

eyes focused on the lines of horizontal pictures, though, until he found himself staring high up at an image of a ship moving across a sea. Ahead of it lay a night sky, a single star near the horizon. The ship seemed to be heading towards it.

Jack reached up and touched the star. He felt a tingle of static electricity, followed by the sound of shifting stones. The wall slid sideways and yellow light flooded into the passage.

Jack and Scarlet stared at what lay beyond.

'New Atlantis,' Scarlet breathed. 'We've found it.'

CHAPTER TWENTY-TWO

An ancient city filled the vast cavern. Columns and porticos, arches and domes stretched all the way to the distant walls. The buildings were made from marble, brass and copper, tarnished green with age. Everything stood at the same height, about fifty feet, except for a single bronze spire, topped with a glass ball, that soared from the centre.

The city was designed in a giant grid about five miles wide. Ivory-coloured cobblestones tiled the streets. Plants choked the avenues, and the trees were unlike anything Jack had ever seen: they looked like palms except the leaves were pale orange and the trunks ash-grey.

Yellow light bathed the cavern. The source of

illumination for the whole city came from mustard-coloured paint on the cave roof. Here and there it had peeled, but it still lit up the city as if it were midday. Where the cavern walls met the ceiling were stone heads with black eyes and round mouths.

No breeze moved the branches on the trees. No water flowed in the aqueducts that ran the length of the metropolis. No people trod the avenues. New Atlantis was completely deserted.

Jack's eyes strayed to the glass ball at the top of the spire. It was slowly changing colour, from blue to red and back to blue.

Was it powered by electricity? Had the ancient Atlanteans found a way to harness that dangerous form of energy?

'Jack,' Scarlet said. 'Where are all the people?'

'I don't know. It looks like no-one's lived here for years. Maybe centuries.'

A stone altar lay below them, and half-a-dozen steps leading into the city. *Blimey*, Jack thought. *We're in some kind of temple.*

At their backs, a huge mural of blue and white stars had been painted on the wall. An immense stone statue stood at each side of the temple, the figures clad in a loose uniform and wearing helmets, shielding their faces.

Jack and Scarlet examined the altar. A dry brown stain, centuries old, painted the stonework.

'Is it—' Jack began.

'Blood.' Scarlet confirmed. 'And lots of it. It's

horrible, but I think there were sacrifices made here.'

'What sort of sacrifices?'

'*Human* sacrifices,' someone said from behind, making Jack and Scarlet jump. 'And many of them.'

The voice came from a small dark man, wearing a cotton smock, standing on a ledge. 'The Old Ones turned to human sacrifice in the end,' he continued, 'and it destroyed them.'

'You stole the Broken Sun!' Jack cried. 'You tried to murder Gloria and Professor Clarke!' He took a step forward, but the stranger pointed a gun, a weapon that looked out of place in the ancient city.

'That was my brother, Andana,' he said. 'And I regret the harm that he caused.'

'Then who are you?' Scarlet demanded.

'My name is Etruba,' he said. 'I am the last of the Atlanteans. My people came here after our city was destroyed ten thousand years ago. We were welcomed as gods by the native people who lived on this island. They helped us build New Atlantis. But we needed more than their help.

'Our gods demanded sacrifices. First we began with the local people. Then we turned to our own. Eventually our beliefs drove us to extinction. Soon there remained only my brother and myself. And now, finally, only me.'

'So your blood rituals destroyed you,' Scarlet said, giving Jack a quick look that said, *I'm playing for time.*

'Why are you still protecting this place?' Jack asked.

'I am awaiting the return of our gods,' Etruba said.

'That time is drawing near.'

Jack looked up at the mural. 'Are they some kind of sky god?'

'Their names are Tsala and Kaleela. They visited us when we were but a simple people, a savage warrior race like those around us. Then they came from the sky and entrusted us with powerful secrets of science. When Tsala and Kaleela left, we continued to develop their sacred technologies, but our ambition outweighed our wisdom. We tried to open a portal into other dimensions, but only succeeded in destroying Atlantis in a single day.'

'But surely you could have just moved to another place and started over,' Scarlet said.

'Yes, but my ancestors were already feared and hated by the other ancient peoples. Many of those other races banded together to wipe us out, so we fled across the seas until, eventually, we hid here and built this new city.'

'But you're still serving these gods,' Scarlet said. 'Why?'

'Because Tsala and Kaleela are soon to return.' Etruba nodded towards the city. 'The mighty spire has begun to glow. It is said that when it shines brighter than the sun, the gods will return.'

As Jack glanced back towards the heart of the city, the ball still slowly changing colour, a gunshot split the air.

A tall man, flanked by two armed guards, had stepped through the mural entrance. He had a face as hard as granite and a large, misshapen nose.

'Allow me to introduce myself,' he called. 'I am

George Darrow and I must thank you all. I never would have found New Atlantis without your assistance.'

George Darrow! The man who visited Clarice's grandfather.

But how does he fit into this mystery?

Etruba stared at the newcomers with hatred. The guards both had their guns trained on him. 'The secrets of Atlantis must not leave the city,' Etruba said. 'That is blasphemy!'

'I'm afraid I can't honour your ancient religion,' Darrow smirked. 'I have my own plans and Atlantean technology will enable me to complete them. Now'—he nodded at the gun in Etruba's hand—'I suggest you lower your weapon.'

'I had hoped there would be no more need for bloodshed.' The Atlantean seemed to be speaking to himself. 'My brother Andana wanted Professor Clarke and the others killed, but I said that too much blood had been spilled over the centuries.'

'Don't be stupid!' Darrow snapped. 'Lower your gun!'

'It is better that Atlantis fall than be handed over to people like you.'

A weapon fired. Jack dragged Scarlet away from the altar. 'Run!' he yelled.

He felt the sting of rock shards as a bullet rebounded off the altar. Scarlet screamed. Jack urged her down the temple steps towards the nearest building. They scrambled around the corner as another bullet ricocheted off the stonework.

'I advise you to return.' Darrow's voice followed them. 'I will make you suffer if you make me look for you.'

Jack steered Scarlet through a nearby doorway. Inside was a living room, its ceiling covered in the same paint as the cavern roof. The table in the centre was stone, but the surrounding chairs were made from some kind of glass.

A quick search revealed no weapon. There was little here in the way of personal possessions. They tore into another room: a bedroom almost as sparse, except for a doll on the bed. A hairbrush made of the same glassy material lay on a stone dressing table. It looked like the owner could return at any moment: it was hard to believe they had been dead for years.

Scarlet urged Jack on, and they scuttled through to a kitchen made up of a strange combination of ancient and modern features. A stone benchtop. Metal cabinets. Saucepans and pots and a glass cooktop.

'The window,' Jack said, pointing.

They climbed through to a small back garden, overgrown with unfamiliar plants and surrounded by a bronze wall. Seeing the vegetation reminded Jack why they had come here in the first place. The Sleeping Death. Phoebe had described it as having a purple thorn and ivory leaves. But nothing here fit that description.

Another shot rang out.

'That sounded close,' Jack said.

'We need to get out.'

'We need to find the plant first. Then we'll find a way out.'

'I don't look forward to going back up those stairs again.'

'There's got to be more than one way out of the city,' Jack said. 'We just need to find it.'

They scrambled over another wall, dropping into a back lane. Their footsteps on the cobblestone streets sounded like a stampede. Zigzagging across several city blocks, they arrived at an outer wall.

'Jack,' Scarlet said quietly. 'Look at that.'

She pointed to a crumpled piece of machinery in the bushes. At first Jack thought it was a sculpture: a strange contraption of metal and bone. Then he looked more closely and realised it was a mechanical frame attached to a skeleton. It had once been a dog. The metal cap now sat loosely on its skull. The outside was smooth, but jagged needles poked from underneath into where the brain would have been. The remainder of the structure was some sort of exoskeleton, a complicated network of gears, pistons and cogs.

'What on earth?'

'It's what Darrow was talking about,' Scarlet said. 'It's a Living Machine.'

'But isn't it a dog?'

'It was, but not anymore. The skull cap must form some sort of interface between the machine and the animal.'

'So this is what Darrow is after. But why?'

'You saw those machine men outside. He must be trying to perfect the process with Atlantean technology.'

'But that's crazy.'

'To us, but not to him.' She looked past Jack. 'Is that a doorway?'

It was a dark crevice in the rock face, nestled behind some orange-leafed trees. Jack and Scarlet raced down the lane.

A figure appeared from around a corner.

Etruba.

He leaned unsteadily against a wall, the gun still in his hand, a patch of blood staining his shirt.

'You should put down that gun,' Jack said. 'You're injured and—'

'I am the last of my people,' Etruba said. 'When I am gone, no-one will remain to safeguard the secrets of the city. Tsala will be angry if he returns to find his people gone and their secrets shared.'

Jack thought it sounded awfully ominous. 'What do you mean?'

'It will be safer for our world if he does not return.'

'What are you going to do?' Scarlet asked.

'What must be done.' Etruba nodded to the exit. 'Go. That way leads out.'

Jack didn't want to leave him to die alone. 'Are you sure?'

'Go!'

They didn't need to be told twice. They ran. Passing

an intersection, a shot rang out, a bullet ricocheting off a nearby wall. One of Darrow's men was behind. Scarlet dragged Jack into a side alley and they kept running, weaving across city blocks.

Jack was disoriented. 'Where—'

'This way.'

Scarlet led him through a house and out the other side. They were close to the cavern wall now where a long pathway stretched in both directions. Trees shrouded an exit. They pushed through the undergrowth and eased the door open to a set of stairs.

Turning back to look once more at New Atlantis, Jack felt a pang of sadness. This great city had been lost for so long. To leave it now…

No!

'I completely forgot!' Jack said. 'The plant!'

'What?'

'The Sleeping Death! We need it to save Gloria and Professor Clarke!'

The ground began to shake. It felt like an earthquake, but it did not subside. Jack's eyes searched the cavern until he spotted Etruba at a temple on the far side. The small man stood in front of a mosaic of a winged chariot, his hands pressed onto one of the hubs.

'He must be activating some sort of machine,' Scarlet said.

'To do what?' Jack asked.

'I'm not sure. It's not to play music.'

A distant roar shook the cavern, growing louder with each passing second. Water shot from the stone heads set high on the walls, the streams crashing into the city like high-power fire hoses, annihilating thousands of years of civilisation.

CHAPTER TWENTY-THREE

'I need to go back,' Jack said. 'You go up the tunnel and find the others.'

'Are you mad?' Scarlet said. 'I'm a woman. Not a potted vase.'

They charged back into the streets. The water was now rising dangerously. Thousands of gallons were pouring in every second. New Atlantis would be swamped within minutes.

'Do you remember seeing an ivory-coloured plant?' Jack asked.

'I don't know,' Scarlet said. 'Was it growing at one of the city squares?'

At the end of the alley they spotted a fountain.

'There!' she yelled. The noise in the cavern was louder than ever. 'Let's try that one!'

Jack cautiously stepped around the cascade of spraying water as they searched the plants at the base of the fountain.

An ivory-coloured plant, Jack thought. *With thorns. An ivory plant with thorns.*

'There's nothing here,' he yelled.

'There's another square!' Scarlet pointed.

They raced to the next fountain. It was like running along the beach at low tide, the water pulling at their ankles. Crossing an intersection, they spotted one of Darrow's men, who shot at them. Scarlet dragged Jack into an open doorway and through the house to another back lane.

After more zigzagging, they reached the city square. By now the water was up to their knees, making every step a struggle. Scarlet's arm shot out.

'There! At the base of the statue.'

They were lucky. A few more minutes and the plant would have been underwater. Its stalks were long and thin, covered in purple thorns. The same used to poison Professor Clarke and Gloria. Jack was no judge of plants, but right now it was the most beautiful thing he had ever seen.

He grabbed handfuls of leaves and stuffed them down his shirt.

'Come on!' he yelled.

As they took off towards the exit, the lighting

system failed, and for one horrible instant, Jack thought they would forever remain in this underground tomb, swallowed by darkness and drowned by rising waters. Then the ceiling flickered back to life.

The water was at their waists as they climbed steps to the crevice in the rock, heading back towards the passageway.

Craaack!

A section of the roof—as large as an elephant—fell, crashing into the city. The light flickered alarmingly, this time only returning to half-power.

Jack looked back to where Etruba had started the self-destruct sequence. The small man lay motionless at the foot of the mural as the water rose around his face and he disappeared under the rising tide.

The chamber shook again, a massive crack forming across the centre of the ceiling.

'Come on,' Scarlet said, grabbing Jack's hand. 'Let's get out of here.'

She dragged him up the stairs. The earth shook violently. What if the tunnel ahead was already collapsed?

Jack gripped the compass in his pocket.

'Almost there,' he said, as much to Scarlet as himself. 'Only a few more feet.'

The lights brightened once more then failed, drowning them in darkness. Jack crashed into Scarlet.

We've still got matches, Jack thought. *We can use them for light. But what if there's no way out at the top? What if Etruba was lying?*

Scarlet nudged him. 'I can see light,' she said. 'Over there.'

They scrambled up the remaining stairs into a small cave, strangely quiet despite the chaos below. Vines and plants shrouded the entrance. Jack and Scarlet tore a hole in the foliage and pushed through into the outside world, fresh air against their faces.

Jack cried out in relief. Bright daylight streamed through the canopy. The smell of the jungle was intoxicating after so many hours underground. Jack felt dizzy with elation as he hugged Scarlet. They were safe.

'Jack,' Scarlet murmured.

'Yes?' He drew back from her.

She was looking past him, her face filled with horror. Jack turned to see armed guards with guns trained on them, the two machine men behind. George Darrow stepped from the shadows.

'Good,' he said, smirking. 'Some new specimens for my experiment.'

Jack and Scarlet were bound and helpless on the ground in minutes. Jack stared up at the machine men. Then he saw dried blood on their arms.

'Where's Mr Doyle?' Jack demanded. 'What have you—'

One of Darrow's henchmen cuffed him across the face and placed a sack over his head. A punch to the stomach then drove the air from his lungs. Desperately trying to breathe, Jack felt metal hands lift him as he was thrown unceremoniously over a machine man's shoulder.

He blacked out. When he next woke, he felt blood on his face and in his eyes. The sack had been pulled off his head. He saw a floor, metal bars and a timber ceiling.

Jack sat up, groaning. The restraints were also gone.

He and Scarlet had been imprisoned in two cells. Bars ran from floor to ceiling. Jack called to Scarlet, but she didn't stir.

A sound came from the door and Jack looked up to see a face watching him through a small window in its centre. The man had grey eyes and a moustache.

Jack leapt to his feet. 'I'll kill you if you've harmed her!' he yelled. 'I swear it.'

'Sure you will, kid.' The man looked bored, as if he'd heard similar threats before. 'Nice to see you're awake. Don't worry: your friend will be fine.'

'Who are you people?' Jack asked.

'You can call me Rick. You don't need to know more than that.'

'Why are you doing this?'

'Why does anyone do anything? It pays well.'

'What are you? Some sort of mercenary?'

'You say that like it's a bad thing.' Rick smirked. 'I'll get Mr Darrow for you.'

The window slid shut. Jack saw a tiny porthole on the other side of the room. Edging towards it, he glimpsed sea, a patch of land, the black balloon of an airship. They were high above the ocean on board the vessel that had attacked the *Explorer*.

Jack called to Scarlet again, and this time she stirred, opening her eyes. 'What happened?' she asked, struggling to her feet. 'Where's my cup of tea?'

'We were captured by Darrow's men.'

'Oh dear.' She rubbed her head. 'That's right. I remember now. Atlantis. Straight from the frying pan...'

'...into the fire,' Jack said. 'I know what you mean.' He was relieved to see Scarlet on her feet, although she did have a nasty lump on her forehead. 'I suppose Blinking Bumblebee has been in a similar situation,' he said. 'Do you recall how she escaped?'

'Ask me when my head isn't about to explode.'

They heard footsteps. Rick unlocked the door and George Darrow entered. This was the first time Jack had seen the man properly. A white scar began at his left ear and ran down to his neck. He wore a dark-green outfit similar to a military uniform, but with no insignia. He smiled without humour, nodding to the porthole.

'Smollett's Island is far behind us. We'll be back in England within days,' he said.

'Where are Mr Doyle and the others?' Jack asked.

'They are dead.'

Jack's vision swam. He tried to speak, but he could not breathe.

Darrow continued. 'My men hunted them down one at a time. Your mentor was the last to fall. A very resourceful man, he was no match—'

'You're lying!' Jack had finally regained the power of speech. 'I don't believe anything you're saying!'

'Suit yourself.'

'Why are we here?' Scarlet asked. 'What's this all about?'

'Those are good questions,' Darrow said. 'And I will give you an equally good explanation. It all began with a little skirmish we now call the Great War.'

'Millions died,' Scarlet said. 'Hardly a skirmish.'

'As you wish. The call went out and we answered. Farmers, labourers, scientists, doctors, all brothers-in-arms, lining up to fight and die on faraway battlefields like cattle in a slaughterhouse.

'We gave our hearts and our lives for the Empire. And what did we get in return? Peace. After years of sacrificing our best and brightest for the Empire, we had a new world order.'

'Everyone made sacrifices,' Jack said.

George Darrow held up a finger. 'That's where you're wrong. How many members of the Royal Family perished? Not one. No, my boy, the Empire demanded the blood and flesh of the common man and we gave it.'

'It was a terrible time,' Jack said. 'Everyone knows that.'

'The greatest difficulty is recognising the true enemy,' Darrow continued. 'Our leaders point into the distance and say there is the enemy.' He clenched his fist. 'But you know who the enemy truly is? Our own government! The leaders who sent us to the slaughter! It was their war! Not ours!' He stopped, took a deep breath. 'Our own government is the enemy. Not distant strangers with whom we have no quarrel.'

'What do you intend to do?' Scarlet asked.

'There must be vengeance,' he said. 'Blood must be repaid with blood.'

CHAPTER TWENTY-FOUR

It was dark. Hours had passed since Darrow had announced his scheme. Jack and Scarlet had seen no other crew member. No food had been delivered. Dividing their emergency supplies, they had eight pieces of beef jerky between them. They ate four, saving the rest. Who knew when their next meal might arrive?

Jack still had all his other belongings. Darrow's men had not bothered searching him. The precious plant retrieved from New Atlantis was stuffed down the front of his shirt. He also had his lock pick, but it was useless: the lock on the outside of the cell was too far away.

Jack couldn't get Darrow's words out of his mind about Mr Doyle.

Your mentor was the last to fall...

'You can't believe him,' Scarlet said. 'Darrow is just trying to demoralise us.'

'He's succeeding,' Jack said.

'This is where you're doing yourself a disservice by not reading the Brinkie Buckeridge books,' Scarlet said. 'Brinkie is often captured by evildoers, but she is never frightened by their taunts. In *The Adventure of the Laughing Boulder*, she was told that Wilbur Dusseldorf has been fed to a tank of hungry turtles and all that remains is his big toe.'

'Scarlet, I'm not sure what part of that story I find the most incredible. That someone would write a book about a giggling boulder—'

'A laughing boulder.'

'—or that someone would get fed to a tank of turtles and all that remains is their—what?'

'Big toe.'

'I don't recall ever seeing Mr Doyle's toes. How will we identify him if only a toe remains?'

'I'm not sure. The police department are just now starting to use fingerprints to catch criminals. I wonder if Mr Doyle has his toeprints on file?'

'What a good question. I'll be sure to print his toes when I see him next. Should I bring it gently into the conversation or just spring it on him? You know, like, "Mr Doyle? Do you mind if I make a print of your toes in case you're ever eaten by giant turtles and all that remains is your big toe?"'

'You make it sound like it's a silly idea,' Scarlet said.

'Not at all. I'm getting my ears printed. And my tongue. Just in case.'

'That's ridiculous.'

Jack sighed. 'I just hope Mr Doyle and the others are all right.'

'So do I.'

There were no beds so they curled up on the floor. Jack reached through the bars, took Scarlet's hand and gave it a squeeze. Hours later, he woke to the steady hum of the airship's engine like a hive of bees in the night.

He listened to Scarlet breathing. She said something in her sleep and rolled over. Jack wondered what their next move should be. Darrow had said they were returning to England. There seemed little chance of getting out of this cell, let alone escaping the airship. All they could do was wait for the right moment to arrive.

And what about Gloria? Was she alive? They had to get the plant to her and Professor Clarke. And Mr Doyle. Was he dead or was George Darrow lying? Jack closed his eyes.

When he opened them next, the early light of day was streaming in the window. Scarlet was already up and trying to peer out the glass from her side of the bars. Jack sat up painfully with a crick in his neck.

'How did you sleep?' he asked.

'Oh,' she said. 'Like a princess.'

'Me too. Er…that is, like a prince.'

Scarlet nodded to the window. 'They've been taking

on supplies at a harbour,' she said. 'I think we're back in Rabat.'

Jack looked out the window and saw city spires. He remembered the wonderful day they had enjoyed with Phoebe. Would they ever see her or Mr Doyle again?

The airship shuddered as the engines came to life. The ship started moving.

'We'll be back in England soon,' Jack said.

They sat down and talked. Jack spoke about his days with his parents. Scarlet was always interested to hear about the sights and sounds of circus life. She gave him the latest news about Brinkie Buckeridge. The annual convention was coming up.

The one topic they did not discuss was food. They had been locked away for more than a day. They still had their four meagre pieces of beef jerky, but Jack wanted to save them.

Late in the morning, their fast ended when Rick appeared with two plates of dry bread and a bottle of water. After stuffing the food in his mouth, Jack asked Rick why he was supporting Darrow.

'I have special skills that make me valuable.' Rick gave a wry smile. 'And I only speak the international language.'

'What's that?'

'Money.'

'You would sell out for money?'

Rick shrugged. 'A man's got to make a living. I'll be long gone by the time the doctor has carried out his plan.'

'When's that happening?'

Rick smiled, waving a finger at him. 'The doctor said you were a smart lad. You don't need to worry about the big day. It won't involve you or your lady friend.'

'So why are we here?'

The smile faded to a sadness so unexpected it sent a chill up Jack's spine. 'I can't say.' He nodded to the bread. 'Eat up, boy. You'll need your strength.'

He departed without another word, leaving Jack and Scarlet to chew on in silence. Jack didn't want to reveal his fears, remembering Darrow's words back on the island.

Some new specimens for my experiment.

What sort of experiment?

Once darkness came, the only light was from the moon, the only sound Scarlet's voice. Jack was glad she was here. He would have hated being locked in this cell with only his thoughts to keep him company.

Just after dawn, Jack was woken by men shouting and the engine changing rhythm. The airship was slowing; it felt like they were landing. Scarlet pointed to the porthole. The stonework of a building flashed by. Men yelled orders about towlines and the ship shuddered before coming to a halt.

'I wonder what happens now,' Scarlet said.

No sooner were the words out of her mouth did Rick enter, flanked by two men. One was tall and thin. His companion shorter, stockily built. Rick introduced them as Leckie and Johnson. They all carried guns.

There was something familiar about Leckie, Jack thought.

'I know you!' he said. 'You were disguised as Professor Clarke!'

'I was wondering if you'd recognise me,' Leckie said, laughing. 'I enjoyed a long career in the theatre, but this sort of work pays far better.'

Jack was worried that Rick was prepared to reveal his men's names. It was as if he didn't expect Jack or Scarlet to ever tell anyone else.

'We don't want any trouble,' Johnson said, revealing a toothless mouth. 'We just have to deliver you to the castle.'

'What's going to happen to us?' Scarlet asked.

'You can ask Mr Darrow about that,' Rick said.

Once again, Jack was sure he caught a troubled expression in Rick's eyes. Jack now thought he knew what was planned—and it wasn't anything good.

Sandwiched between the men, Jack and Scarlet were led a short distance through the airship and down a gangplank. They were moored next to a castle, somewhere off the east coast of Scotland, Jack guessed.

'Keep moving,' Leckie said, jabbing him with his gun.

They were taken into the turret and down a spiral staircase. The cold building closed in, the walls wet with moisture. The place smelt dusty and dank. Passing a window slit, Jack caught sight of a collapsed stone structure, and at the bottom of the stairs they were pushed down a corridor, dimly lit by gaslights.

We haven't seen anyone else other than Darrow and these few men, Jack thought.

'Where's the rest of your crew?' he asked.

'The *Avenger* is almost completely automated,' said Rick. 'It's his own design. I've never seen anything like it. Takes less than half-a-dozen men to operate.'

'That's amazing.' They seemed to be moving away from the shore. 'I thought he had an entire garrison at his disposal,' Jack said.

Leckie answered. 'He doesn't need them with those machine men.'

'Best stay quiet about 'em,' Johnson warned.

'No harm,' Leckie said, ignoring him. 'Those machine men will sort anyone out. One of them's worth both houses—'

'Shut up,' Rick snapped.

They reached a thick timber door. Rick unlocked it, revealing a lengthy room lit by a square window high up on one stone wall. The area had been divided into cells with a corridor down the middle. Each of the cells contained a man, either drugged or asleep, lying on beds.

Jack and Scarlet were shoved into the nearest cell.

'Our work here is finished.' Rick gave them a brief nod. 'Hope all goes well for you.'

'What's going to happen to us?' Jack asked.

Leckie started. 'The doctor has some rather interesting plans—'

'I said shut up,' Rick snapped. Turning to Jack, he said, 'Just do as the doctor says and you'll be fine.'

The men locked the cell and left. Around the room there were a dozen men, each of them ghostly pale, as if they had not seen sunlight for years. They all seemed disabled in some way, missing arms or legs.

They were dressed in the same makeshift uniform that Darrow had been wearing. Their hair was cut short and they were clean-shaven.

'What is this place?' Scarlet asked.

'I don't know. Something to do with Darrow's experiments.'

'Is this…' Scarlet swallowed and clenched her fists. 'Is this what he has planned for us?'

Jack shuddered. Why would Darrow amputate someone's arms or legs? It made no sense. Was he some kind of Doctor Frankenstein?

A man shifted on one of the bunks. Both his legs were gone below the knees; his eyes were hollow, ringed by dark circles. Easing himself onto the edge of the bunk, he gazed about in a daze.

Scarlet drew breath. 'Oh no,' she said. 'It's not possible.'

'What is it?' Jack asked.

'We know that man.'

'What?' Jack looked at the legless man. 'I've never seen him before in my life.'

'You have,' Scarlet said. 'His portrait hangs above the fireplace at Amelia Doyle's house. That's Mr Doyle's son—Phillip Doyle.'

CHAPTER TWENTY-FIVE

Jack stared hard at the man, trying to remember the pictures of Phillip. Other than the portrait at his family home, there was also the old photograph of him as a child, with his parents back at Bee Street.

'Bazookas,' Jack murmured. 'I think you're right.'

The man *looked* like Mr Doyle. He could have been a younger version of the great detective.

Phillip was in a cell on the other side of the passage-way. Jack went to the bars and pushed his face through. 'Phillip? Can you hear me?'

The man did not reply, only stared wordlessly into space. Jack and Scarlet called his name several more times, but he either didn't hear or wasn't interested in replying.

Some other men in the cells sat up and stared, but like Phillip they remained silent, lost in their own worlds.

Another man in the next cell, who was missing arms, spoke up. 'The government must pay,' he said. 'The criminals are the men of Westminster.'

'What is your name?' Scarlet asked. 'Who are you?'

'Betrayals must be repaid.' His face twitched. 'The blood of the innocent will be avenged.'

'Please,' Jack said. 'We want to help you.'

The stranger lay back down on his bunk, his lips moving as if reading words on the ceiling.

'What's wrong with them?' Jack asked Scarlet.

'I don't know. It's as if their minds have been affected.'

'From the war?'

'Possibly. Many men were left shell shocked from battle. They suffered a kind of mental trauma from the stress of being in such a terrible environment.'

'But what are they doing here?' Jack asked. 'They should be in a hospital.'

'Could they be part of Darrow's plan?' Scarlet's eyes went wide. 'Could they be the men he uses in his machines?'

'They must be! Darrow must have kidnapped them from the battlefields and brainwashed them.'

The thought was horrible. If Jack was right, these men had been kept in captivity for years. Injured in battle and scarred by their experiences in the war, they has been brought here to further manipulate their minds.

'What will we do?' Jack asked.

'First things first,' Scarlet replied. 'Let's get out of here.' She produced her lock pick and undid the cell door.

Jack crossed to Phillip's cell, placing his face near the bars.

'Phillip,' he said. 'My name is Jack. I'm a friend of your father. I want you to come with us.'

Phillip had been staring unfocused at the floor. His eyes now shifted to the ceiling. 'Father,' he whispered.

'Jack,' Scarlet said, gently touching his arm. 'We can't take Phillip.' She motioned to his damaged legs. 'Not without a wheelchair.'

'Phillip,' Jack called. 'Can you move? Can you travel with us?'

But he still didn't answer.

'We're coming back for you, Phillip,' Jack said. 'We'll get you out of here. Your father is waiting. He's been waiting for years.'

'Jack.' Scarlet pulled at his arm. 'We have to go.'

Jack turned to all the men. 'We're coming back for you. You're going home. You're all going home.'

Scarlet had eased open the door and peered through. A man sat on the other side, reading a newspaper. Leckie.

'Excuse me,' Jack said.

Leckie looked up in amazement.

'Is this the way to Piccadilly Circus?' Jack punched him in the chin and knocked him unconscious to the ground. Jack picked up his gun.

'Jack,' Scarlet said.

'What?'

'You know what your aim is like.'

He handed over the weapon. While Mr Doyle did not allow them to carry firearms, he had let them practise in a shooting range. Jack had hit the ceiling, floor and walls more times than the target. Scarlet was a far better shot.

'Just don't shoot my foot off,' he said.

She checked the gun. 'I'm not making any promises.'

Jack led them in the other direction, following the corridor until it turned, ending at an oak door. A small window, laced with bars, was set into it. Beyond lay an overgrown path. And freedom.

'This looks good,' Jack said.

Scarlet pushed against it. 'It looks good, but it's not opening. It's bolted on the other side.'

A distant shout echoed down the tunnel.

'Oh dear,' Scarlet said. 'They've found Leckie.'

Jack gave the door a shove. 'I might be able to get this open if you can buy us some time.'

Scarlet went back to the turn in the tunnel to keep a lookout as Jack threw his shoulder against the door. The sound of men's voices grew closer. 'I advise you not to proceed any further,' Scarlet called to them. 'I am armed with a weapon and prepared to use it.'

The sound of laughter rang down the tunnel.

'You're a nice girl,' Johnson yelled back. 'Why don't you put that gun down before you hurt yourself?'

'Why don't you come and take it?'

A gunshot followed and a man started screaming.

'*She shot me! She shot me in the leg!*'

'I'll aim for your eyes next time!'

Scarlet continued firing as Jack redoubled his efforts with the door. 'I think you'd better hurry,' she said.

She was running out of bullets.

Jack's shoulder was starting to ache and it didn't look like the door was going to give way anytime soon. *You've got to open*, he thought. *Come on. Come on!*

Craaack!

'Scarlet,' he yelled. 'Quickly!'

They tumbled out into bright sunlight. Jack breathed the air in deeply, but there was no time to relax. An old bench was nearby. Jack closed the door and jammed it against the handle.

They raced away down a path into some dense woods. The coast was only a few minutes away. Jack glanced back at Scarlet. Her cheeks were flushed, the wind ran through her red hair, but she wore an expression of grim determination. Her eyes met his.

'Blinkie would be proud of you,' he said.

'It's Brinkie, you idiot!' she yelled and they both laughed.

A small bay came into view with a dock and a few boats tied up at it. A man was just coming in on a small steamboat and, as they raced up the pier, he started to reach into his jacket.

'Don't!' Scarlet snapped, waving the gun at him. 'Get in the water!'

The man took one look at her and jumped into the bay.

Climbing into a boat, Jack quickly worked out the controls and accelerated away from the pier.

'I thought you were going to shoot him,' Jack said.

'With what?' she asked. 'I'm out of bullets.'

Jack brought the engine to full throttle as Scarlet fed coal to the furnace. They were soon out of the bay and into the channel heading for the coast. Jack glanced back. A larger ship was in pursuit.

'Wave your gun,' Jack said. 'Pretend you're going to shoot them.'

'I don't know if this is achieving anything,' she yelled. 'But it makes me feel better.'

He kept their small boat at full throttle, but the other ship, with its bigger engine, continued to gain. They heard an explosion and a whistle, and something whizzed over their bow.

'That was a cannonball,' Scarlet yelled.

Jack swung the wheel around, zigzagging the boat so they presented a more difficult target. Another cannonball sailed through the air. The ship was growing closer with every passing second.

'We're not going to make it!' Jack said. 'Do you have any ideas?'

'There was a Brinkie Buckeridge story where she attached a bomb to a dead body and floated it towards an oncoming ship!' Scarlet shouted. 'It acted as a mine, blowing it to pieces.' Jack stared at her, speechless.

'You said you wanted suggestions! I didn't say it was a good one!'

Again, Jack swung the boat about. 'Hang on!' he said. 'And be ready for anything.'

'Certainly, but we're now heading directly towards the other ship.'

'I know. We're on a collision course.'

'I've heard of captains going down with their ships, but this is ridiculous.'

'Get ready to jump.'

The ship fired its cannon and this time it slammed into their bow. Timber exploded in all directions and their small craft lurched to one side. Scarlet was thrown to the floor as Jack hung onto the wheel, trying to keep them aimed at the other craft.

'Get ready to jump!' Jack cried. 'Now! Jump! *Jump!*'

Jack and Scarlet leapt into the water as the oncoming ship fired another cannonball that sliced through their deck. But nothing could stop their boat's forward momentum.

Cra-ash!

Jack surfaced to see the pursuing vessel listing badly with a football-sized hole in its side.

Scarlet bobbed in the water next to him. 'Not as good as the exploding body,' she said. 'But it will suffice.'

'We need to swim for it,' Jack said. 'They'll be on us in a minute if they don't sink.'

Scarlet peered doubtfully at the coast. 'It's still a mile away.'

'There's no other choice.'

The water was freezing. Their clothing made swimming difficult. Jack considered ditching his green coat, but he wasn't prepared to lose the portrait of his parents or his compass.

He glanced back to see their little fishing boat disappear beneath the waves. The other ship was now aimed in their direction.

'Jack!' Scarlet yelled. 'They're not slowing.'

The ship was now so close that Jack could see the man behind the wheel. It was Leckie.

'He's going to run us over!' Jack cried.

CHAPTER TWENTY-SIX

A great shadow fell over them. *This is it*, Jack thought. *This is how it ends.*

But the ship didn't slam into him. Instead, shots rang out and Jack looked up to see blue sky and an enormous silver balloon with the name *Enforcer* emblazoned on the side.

'It's Scotland Yard!' Scarlet yelled. 'And they're armoured.'

The *Enforcer* swept in low over the water, aimed a cannonball and fired. The ship exploded. Jack and Scarlet ducked as debris splashed all around them. What remained sank within seconds.

'Good heavens,' Scarlet said.

'I think we're saved,' Jack said. 'But who…?'

The airship descended and a window slid across. Three heads simultaneously appeared.

'Mr Doyle!' Jack yelled.

'And Clarice and Phoebe!' Scarlet said.

Jack and Scarlet scrambled up a metal rung ladder. Cheers erupted on board.

'How did you find us?' Jack asked. 'Where have you been?'

'We did a quick spin of the art gallery first,' Mr Doyle said, his eyes twinkling. 'Then a trip over to Brighton Pier. Fed the seagulls and…'

'Ignatius!' Phoebe said. 'Don't tease them!'

'Then I will be concise. Thanks to the efforts of Mr Spaulding and his men, we all escaped. Tobias Bradstreet, Kip and Tan were shot, but will live. Likewise, the crew of the *Explorer* survived the crash into the sea. Many were injured, but made it to shore before the vessel sank in shallow waters.

'At first, all seemed grim as we tried to find you. Then we sighted Darrow's airship leaving the island. We found your tracks and realised you had been taken.'

'But how did you escape the island?' Scarlet asked.

'You recall the equipment on board the *Explorer*?'

'Of course.'

'And what was stored in the hull?'

Jack thought for a moment. 'You don't mean—'

Mr Doyle nodded. 'The submersible. Phoebe is an excellent diver, as it turns out. She was able to dive to the wreck, causing the submersible to surface. We made it operational with the help of Mr Bradstreet and his remarkable crew.'

'But you couldn't make it back to England in the submersible.'

'No, that distance is too great. We were, however, able to reach the African coast. From there we hired an airship—'

'—and that's how you got back to England.'

'Exactly.'

'But how did you find us?'

'Fortunately, thanks to Clarice, we had the name of George Darrow. I had also taken note of the registration number on the side of his airship. We contacted Scotland Yard upon our return—and here we are.' Ignatius Doyle grew serious. 'Unfortunately Professor Clarke and Gloria are still afflicted by the Sleeping Death. Their prognosis is not good.'

'Wait!' Jack cried out so suddenly that everyone jumped, even Mr Doyle. 'I have the plant!'

'The plant?' Phoebe's eyes grew wide.

'We found New Atlantis!' he yelled, dragging the remains of the ivory leaves from his shirt.

'What?' Phoebe gasped. 'Tell me! What was it like?'

'That can wait,' Mr Doyle said. 'We need to get this plant to the hospital immediately.'

The hold of the *Enforcer* contained a small runabout that could start back to London as soon as possible. A pilot was assigned, and Phoebe offered to accompany Clarice on the journey.

After they departed, Scarlet turned to Mr Doyle and said, 'We have some rather important news.'

'What is it?' he asked.

Jack briefly described their journey to Smollett's Island and what they found in the underground cells. 'And Mr Doyle,' he finally said. 'We found Phillip.'

The detective went pale. 'You've both been through a lot...'

'He was in one of the cells,' Scarlet said firmly. 'Phillip is alive.'

'We're not crazy,' Jack said. He went on to explain the condition of the men and the theory that they had been brainwashed. 'I don't know what Darrow's intentions are, but he is planning something.'

'It...it's almost too much to take in,' Mr Doyle said. 'We must journey to the island and rescue Phillip and those men.'

The airship came in to land a small distance from the castle. A police sergeant by the name of Brock appeared and told them to wait while he and his men did a sweep. Several minutes later, he returned.

'The castle appears to be empty,' he said. 'But one of my men reported seeing a black airship heading towards the mainland.'

'They must have left around the far side of the island as we arrived,' Mr Doyle said. 'Are you sure there's no-one at the castle?'

'What about downstairs?' Scarlet asked. 'In the basement?'

'We found a room filled with cells,' Brock said. 'But all the doors were open and the cells empty.'

'So Darrow has escaped,' Mr Doyle said. 'And he's taken Phillip and the other men with him.'

They made their way to the castle where they met with Inspector Greystoke from Scotland Yard.

'What have you found so far?' Mr Doyle asked.

'Very little,' the inspector said. 'I think this is only one of Darrow's bases. There are notes about two other sites in England.'

'So you've found nothing?'

'There *was* evidence of illegal Darwinist experiments in the basement.'

'What sort of experiments?'

The inspector shuddered. 'Hideous things. Snake-rats. Dogs with double rows of teeth. Some had to be put down immediately because of their deformities.'

'Was there any machinery?' Scarlet asked. 'The men on the island wore exoskeletons.'

'We've seen nothing like that. That research must have occurred elsewhere.' He paused, studying Mr Doyle. 'You may wish to sit this one out, Ignatius.'

'What do you mean?'

'We've found a room where the men were brain-washed. It's...unpleasant.'

Mr Doyle took a deep breath. 'I need to see what my son endured,' he said. 'I have to know.'

It was a dungeon at the other end of the castle, with walls covered in photographs taken from the battle-field: images of men lying dead and wounded in muddy trenches.

A phonograph player and a pile of records were positioned at the front with a chair fitted to restrain arms and legs. A slide projector, the same used at magic lantern shows at the theatre, sat in the middle of the room.

Inspector Greystoke played a record. It crackled before George Darrow spoke loud and clear from the bell-shaped horn:

The government is our enemy. It must be made to pay. Revenge must be taken for the crimes against our people. Only through attacking the people responsible…

Greystoke turned it off.

'People have experimented with mind control for years,' Mr Doyle said, slumping into a chair. 'Rarely has it succeeded.'

'We think Darrow may have been drugging the men as well,' the inspector said. 'There are empty vials of medication in a rubbish bin. Darrow's family has been involved in the pharmaceutical industry for years.'

'My dear son…' Mr Doyle's chin quivered as he drew on an inner strength. 'But I must stay focused. Show me the cells where the men were kept.'

A few minutes later, Jack and Scarlet found

themselves back in the chamber where they had so recently been guests. Mr Doyle took them to one side. 'I must ask you once more,' he said. 'Are you sure it was Phillip?'

Jack and Scarlet nodded, then took turns describing the man in the cell, doing their best to be positive about his condition.

'Do either of you have any idea where Darrow may have gone? The involvement of Scotland Yard will likely force his hand.'

'One of the mercenaries made a rather strange comment,' Scarlet said.

Jack agreed. 'He said about the machine men being able to destroy two houses.'

'Two houses?' Mr Doyle said.

'No,' Scarlet said. 'He referred to them as *both* houses.'

Mr Doyle stroked his chin. 'Today the British Parliament—Westminster—is holding a special session to celebrate the King's birthday.'

Jack was confused. 'What does that have to do with people's homes?' he asked.

'Not people's homes,' Mr Doyle said. 'Houses. The British Parliament is comprised of two of them—the House of Commons and the House of Lords. Legislation must pass both houses before it comes into law.'

Inspector Greystoke joined them. 'It would be the ideal opportunity for Darrow to strike at the heart of the British government.' He turned to Mr Doyle. 'How deadly are these machine men?'

'Extremely. One alone is equal to a battalion of men. They are fast and efficient. It was only because we were able to scatter and hide that we escaped.'

'I'm privy to some of the security arrangements for this afternoon,' Greystoke said. 'I know the guard has been doubled because of the King's attendance.'

'They'll need more than that,' Jack said. 'Much more. A dozen machine men would be unstoppable.'

'When does the session begin?' Mr Doyle asked.

'Five o'clock.' Greystoke glanced at his watch. 'We've got a little over four hours.'

They returned to the *Enforcer*. As they flew towards the coast, one of the Scotland Yard men rustled up some cold beef sandwiches.

'I've been thinking about the machine men,' Scarlet said. 'They would appear to be quite indestructible, but I know how to bring them down.'

'What do you have in mind?' Jack asked.

'We need to appeal to their human side.'

'If you say so.'

Mr Doyle was nodding. 'I believe you're right, my dear,' he said. 'Darrow may have done his best to reduce these men to unthinking machines, but they are still men. Human. Fallible. They are still *free* men. His techniques must have been only partly successful, because he wanted the secrets of the living machine from New Atlantis.'

'Why does Darrow hate England so much?' Jack asked.

The detective sighed. 'For some people the war never ends. Living the peace is just as difficult as fighting the war.'

They didn't speak again until London came into view. The airship joined a line of vessels entering the city, peeling off as they came within view of the Houses of Parliament.

The area was under lockdown. Twenty airships crisscrossed the sky. Most of them were police vessels, but several were military.

Soon the information of the threat was being relayed to the whole fleet. One airship broke formation and made its way to them. The vessels descended to the roof of an administration suite.

Inspector Greystoke met with an officer of the other ship. 'That was Warren Timms from the Parliamentary Guard,' he explained on his return. 'He's contacting the relevant government representatives to inform them of the situation.'

'And what are they doing?' Mr Doyle asked.

'Nothing, so far.'

'Surely the event can be cancelled.'

'Not without evidence that an attack is imminent.'

'But can't—'

'Threats are made against the government every day,' the inspector pointed out. 'This is just one of many.'

'Can my team and I be allowed into the building?'

Greystoke promised to arrange access. The airship then took everyone to a parking lot west of the new House of Commons. Old warehouses lined the opposite bank of the Thames. Jack glanced at the names: the Midas Building, Old Oak Industries, Crane Manufacturing. There were crowds of onlookers too, eager to catch a glimpse of the King.

Greystoke returned with security cards that gave them access to the whole building. Then he reboarded the airship.

'We have an issue,' Mr Doyle said as the vessel rose back into the sky. 'The new Parliament has hundreds of rooms and miles of corridors. Do either of you have any idea how we should conduct such a search?'

'Uh, very quickly?' Jack suggested.

'I would suggest you both start at the lower levels and work your way up. The kitchen is down there. I will start at the top and work my way down.'

'Mr Doyle,' Scarlet said, 'that will take days.'

'We must try.' The detective frowned. 'Don't forget: alert the authorities if you see anything suspicious. And don't split up!'

Jack and Scarlet made their way to the elevators. Security guards were everywhere. It was impossible to travel fifty feet without a soldier or officer from Scotland Yard checking their credentials.

They reached the kitchen. It was the largest Jack had ever seen, with benches, ovens and cooking equipment stretching as far as the eye could see. Hundreds of people were busy preparing meals.

Jack led Scarlet through the melee of people chopping and cutting and yelling orders until they reached a quieter corner. A girl, her name badge identifying her as Betty, was pouring cream into a multitude of white jugs.

'I'm with security,' Jack said, trying to sound important. 'Er, have you seen anything strange?'

'Strange?' She glanced up at him, but continued to pour. 'In what way?'

Jack wasn't sure how he could describe a dozen machine men.

'Just odd,' he said lamely.

'I *have* seen something strange.'

'Really?' Scarlet said. 'What?'

'You two.' Betty, frowned at them. 'You're the only people here not working.'

They took the hint and kept moving. Jack continued to scan the kitchen. At first, the place had appeared completely chaotic, but now he realised that everyone was simply busy; they knew what they had to do and were doing it.

Then an older blonde woman passed by a shelf at the end of the chamber and disappeared through a rear door. Jack only saw her for a second, but his heart gave a lurch.

That's not possible, he thought. *She's dead.*

But he was sure it was her.

Sandra Clegg.

CHAPTER TWENTY-SEVEN

'Bazookas,' Jack said. 'That was Sandra Clegg!'

'Are you sure?' Scarlet asked.

Was it really her? Or had he mistaken one of the cooks for Clegg? It had been an exhausting few days. He described the woman to Scarlet. 'I'm not positive,' he said. 'But it looked like her.'

'She's doing very well for a dead woman,' Scarlet said. 'She has a new job and a flashy hairstyle.'

'Now you're the one being silly. If you'd—'

The building shook. The kitchen staff stopped almost as one. Someone dropped a stack of plates and they shattered. Two security guards appeared, charging past Jack and Scarlet.

'It sounds like an attack on the upper levels,' one said to the other. 'Lock down the elevators and keep them secure.'

Jack was inclined to follow, but remembered Sandra. His stomach churned. Whatever was happening on the upper floors could be a diversion. Maybe the real action was about to happen *under* Parliament.

One of the chefs yelled for work to continue. Jack turned around, almost knocked over a man with a plate of small pies, and went to the doorway where the woman had disappeared.

'Where are you going?' Scarlet asked.

'I'm not sure.'

Jack grabbed the arm of a young boy carrying a box.

'Where does that corridor lead?' Jack asked.

'Nowhere. It used to be dry storage, but they had a problem with rising damp.'

The boy headed off and Scarlet turned to Jack. 'So we're chasing a ghost?' she asked. 'Shouldn't we go upstairs?'

'They've got plenty of people upstairs. This may be important.'

Leaving the noisy kitchen, Scarlet followed him down the corridor. The silence closed in around them. They were underground, and it was cold. Water stains discoloured the walls.

'Moisture must be seeping in from the Thames,' Scarlet said.

The corridor wound about to stairs leading down.

A lamp set into the wall at the bottom cast a feeble glow.

'I hate to say it,' Scarlet said, 'but this reminds me of a Brinkie Buckeridge novel.'

'There's one for all occasions, isn't there?'

'It's *The Adventure of the Drinking Nose*.'

'I won't even ask how that's possible.'

'She goes down a flight of stairs with her Peruvian guide. When they get to the bottom, the door at the top closes behind them and a beehive drops from the ceiling, releasing thousands of killer bees.'

'And what happens?'

'Brinkie survives.'

'And the Peruvian guide?'

'Uh…well.'

At the bottom was a padlock on the door. Secured. Sandra—if that was who she was—could not have come this way.

'I think I've led us on a wild goose chase.'

'Or a wild cook chase, except…'

Scarlet gripped the lock and shook it. It was secure, but a lock was only as effective as the screws holding it in place and *these were gone*. Open mouthed, Scarlet pulled the hinge back and pushed the door open to reveal a gloomy interior.

The smell of mould was strong, almost overpowering. Empty shelves lined both walls. The boy from the kitchen had been correct in saying the storage room was no longer used. Stepping into the murky chamber, they started down the aisle.

Suddenly, a gun was rammed into the back of Jack's head.

'I'd advise you not to move,' a voice said. 'I don't want to kill you, but I will if I must.'

'Sandra?' Scarlet said.

The woman rounded on them with the weapon in her hand. 'This is quite a surprise,' she said. 'You two have more lives than a cat.'

'We might say the same thing about you.'

'If you stay quiet and do as I say, you might survive this in one piece,' Sandra said.

'Why are you doing this? Surely you're not in favour of attacking the Houses of Parliament?'

'I'm doing what must be done.'

'Murdering innocent people?' Jack asked. 'How can that be right?'

'Murder is wrong,' she agreed. 'Just as murdering my sons was wrong.' Her chin trembled, but she did not lower the gun. 'They had names—Reggie, Anthony and Edwin. They were people. Now they're lying in a field in France. Forever lost.'

'Your sons…'

'My real name is Darrow.' She smiled sadly. 'You didn't really think my name was Clegg, did you? The government took the lives of a generation. Good men who deserved better than they got.'

'But the war was years ago,' Scarlet said. 'Why now?'

'George wanted the injured men to help him of their own free will.'

'But when that didn't work he tried to brainwash them.'

Sandra hesitated. 'I know it wasn't right,' she said. 'George wanted the technology from New Atlantis to finalise his work, but it's too late now. It's only a matter of time before we're caught.'

'Then give up,' Scarlet said. 'There's no need for bloodshed.'

'There has already been blood,' Sandra said, darkly. 'Now it must be repaid.'

She swung the gun, striking Jack across the temple.

When he opened his eyes again, his head hurt and the air was filled with dust and debris. Broken shelves lay everywhere. A few lights feebly illuminated the storage room. There had been an explosion. Turning his head, he saw Scarlet on the floor next to him, her eyes fluttering open.

They had been dragged to the far end of the chamber. Voices echoed through the gloom. Standing at the edge of a hole, Sandra had the gun trained on them. There was a railway track below, the metal rails twisted by the blast.

A dozen machine men appeared in the tunnel. Jack and Scarlet huddled in terror as they climbed through the gap. One carried George Darrow on his shoulders as easily as a father might carry a small boy.

Darrow was lowered to the floor, his eyes fixed on Jack and Scarlet. 'What are they doing here, Mother?' he asked. 'Why are they still alive?'

Sandra's face twisted with confusion. 'They're just children,' she said. 'Surely they don't have to die too.'

'If they're not with us, they're against us.'

Jack's eyes searched the masks of the machine men until he focused on one. The man was almost identical to the others: covered in body armour, an engine attached to his back, guns and grenade launchers strapped to his arms. But there was something familiar about him.

'Phillip Doyle!' Jack said. 'Do you remember us? We know your father!'

George Darrow laughed. 'You think these men are so easily swayed? They have sworn to follow my every command. Within hours the prime minister, the entire Cabinet and the King will be dead. The men who caused the war will pay with their own blood.'

'It will not be as easy as you believe.'

The voice came not from Darrow but the shadows behind Jack and Scarlet, as Mr Doyle broke from the gloom.

'I have alerted the authorities to your attack and the building is being evacuated as we speak. We know the automated attacks from your airship were simply a diversion. There are hundreds of soldiers ready to defend this building—with their lives, if necessary.'

'Then they will pay with their lives,' Darrow snarled.

'George,' Sandra said, lowering the gun. 'We can't do that. They're not our enemy!'

'They are all our enemies!' Darrow snapped. 'We'll fight to the last man!'

Mr Doyle's eyes focused on a machine man. 'Phillip?' he said. 'Can you hear me? It's your father.'

'You are dead to him,' Darrow said.

'I searched for you on the field after the battle,' Mr Doyle said to his son. 'I tried to find you, but you were gone. This man took you away—'

'Ignore him!' Darrow said to Phillip. 'He is our enemy!'

'—from me and Amelia and Jason,' Mr Doyle persisted. 'You remember them, don't you, Phillip? You remember how you and I used to play when you were a boy? All the fun we used to have.'

'Prove your loyalty to me, Phillip!' Darrow demanded, pointing at Mr Doyle. 'Kill him!'

Phillip raised his arms.

'No!' Sandra cried.

She made a grab for her son, but he knocked her to the ground.

'I'm giving you an order, soldier,' Darrow told Phillip. 'You're going to kill that man. He betrayed you! He betrayed his country!'

Confusion crossed Phillip Doyle's face.

'We had so many good times,' Mr Doyle continued. 'You remember your mother and the games we used to play? The songs we used to sing?'

'He's the enemy!' Darrow cried. 'Destroy him!'

Phillip pointed his arms at his father. The engines whirred as grenade launchers locked into place.

Mr Doyle started to sing. '*The Minstrel Boy will*

return we pray. When we hear the news we all will cheer it—'

'Kill him!' Darrow screamed. 'Kill him!'

The confusion cleared in Phillip's eyes. He looked about as if waking from a dream, saw the devastation in the room, the machine men, Jack and Scarlet and finally his father.

Darrow seethed with hatred. 'If you won't kill him,' he cried, spittle lacing his chin, 'I will!'

Darrow produced a revolver. At the same time, Phillip's eyes narrowed. A bittersweet smile played on his lips as he lifted his arms high, training his guns on the ceiling. Firing them would bring the whole roof down.

'Run!' Mr Doyle cried. He dragged Jack and Scarlet towards the back of the room. Jack saw George Darrow fire his gun at Phillip and the bullet *ting* harmlessly off his armour.

'No!' Darrow screeched, terror in his voice. 'No!'

Phillip Doyle fired the grenade launchers into the ceiling.

Woompf!

Everything moved in slow motion. Jack was airborne, catapulted through the air by the blast. He hit the ground and rolled. Scarlet and Mr Doyle went sprawling. Choking through the dust, Jack looked back to see the ceiling sagging precariously.

Phillip Doyle gave them a final nod. Then the building itself seemed to moan in pain as the ceiling collapsed.

A wall of dust and debris swept towards Jack as night closed in, a night without stars or moonlight, as if the whole world had been buried alive.

CHAPTER TWENTY-EIGHT

'I need to know everything,' Gloria said. 'Every last detail.'

A month had passed since the collapse in the basements of new Parliament. The building had been evacuated, and Mr Doyle and the team rescued by firemen. They had sustained minor cuts and lacerations from the explosions and falling debris.

There had been good news waiting for them at the hospital. The medication synthesised from the Sleeping Death plant had been successful in waking Gloria and Professor Clarke. Since then, the receptionist had spent weeks slowly regaining her strength before rejoining them at Bee Street. She was still dangerously thin, but the colour had at least returned to her face.

Now she was curled up on the lounge in the sitting room surrounded by pillows and blankets, ready to write up the case file, notepad in hand. Mr Doyle, Jack and Scarlet had been obeying her every whim. Jack had the feeling she was enjoying the attention—and he didn't mind at all.

'It's rather a long story,' Mr Doyle said. 'Are you sure you're up for it?'

'You're treating me too much like an invalid,' she said. 'Oh, but do pass the cream biscuits.'

'Well,' Mr Doyle paused. 'Where will I start?'

'At the beginning,' Gloria suggested.

'Then we must begin with the war,' he sighed. 'George Darrow was a doctor during the conflict. He worked on the battlefields before being transferred to head up a convalescence unit. One of his duties was to ship men back home to recover from their injuries. England was desperate for doctors, so the authorities were not concerned with Darrow or his past.

'If they had checked, they would have realised he had already been dismissed from two hospitals as well as the Darwinist League for illegal practices.'

'That explains the bulls I found in the basement in Southwold,' Jack said.

'Indeed.' Mr Doyle stroked his chin. 'I do believe, however, that when George Darrow first arrived in France, he genuinely wanted to help. He undoubtedly saved many lives.'

'So what went wrong?' Gloria asked.

'The war went wrong,' Mr Doyle said. 'Darrow's brothers were killed. All three of them. It didn't happen at once. Rather, over a period of months, he lost them. You can understand the effect it must have had; each of them dying while he remained alive.'

'And Sandra Darrow, his mother?'

'She was in England, helping Darrow run the hospital. After the loss of his youngest brother, he started evacuating men from the field and sending them back to England under false names.'

'Why?'

Mr Doyle paused. 'It's impossible to say exactly when he grew to hate our country. Regardless, at some point he decided to take revenge by using veterans as soldiers for his exoskeleton experiments.'

'But...' Gloria didn't have the words. 'Using men who had already lost so much? Using men who were themselves victims?'

'These men were traumatised. In a way, they were the ideal recipients for Darrow's brainwashing techniques: they were already addled, their minds in a state of shock and confusion. To twist them to his way of thinking was a shorter leap than for someone of sound mind.'

'And the exoskeletons themselves?' Gloria asked. 'Where did they spring from?'

'The body armour for the machine men was already being built by Darrow's father prior to the war. He was a genius. Not only a brilliant chemist, he was also an engineer. He died just as the suits were completed.'

'But the brainwashing process was not perfect?'

'No. The men would carry out Darrow's orders, but would falter at inopportune times. Darrow needed them compliant to his every command. When he heard about the legend of the Living Machine, he realised the ancient Atlanteans had exactly what he needed.'

Scarlet spoke up. 'It's ironic that his desire for revenge led to the discovery of New Atlantis,' she said. 'And, tragically, the city was destroyed.'

'A terrible historical loss, but we are fortunate that Darrow's secrets of mind control were also lost. He and his mother were the only ones who knew their techniques, and they died in the basement collapse.'

'I'll take freedom any day,' Jack said.

'How did Sandra Clegg—I mean, *Darrow*—fit into all this?' Gloria asked. 'She was helping her son, yet she seemed adverse to violence.'

'I believe it was Sandra who sent the watch to Amelia,' Mr Doyle said. 'Later, she wrote to us about the British Museum. I think she was torn between helping her son and doing what she felt was right.

'She knew that George Darrow was building up to an attack on the government and possibly the disabled men in his care would be hurt or killed.

'After the house in Southwold burnt down, she made some enquiries and realised her good deed had brought me into the case. Later, when Smythe joined the crew as the first mate, she enlisted as cook. I think

George Darrow wanted them both there in case one was discovered.

'On the island, Sandra slipped away, leaving a scrap of blood-soaked fabric to make it look like she'd been taken by a wild animal.'

'How did she end up at the Houses of Parliament?' Gloria asked.

'There was no subterfuge involved there. She had already worked in the kitchens of new Parliament for years. On the day of the attack, she was required to drug the guards. With them out of the way, it left clear access for the machine men to enter the building.'

'And how did you end up on the scene when Darrow broke in? What made you realise he intended attacking from underground?'

'I had begun my rather fruitless search on the roof of new Parliament when I happened to glance across the river. There were several dilapidated warehouses on the other side. One of them was a building bearing the sign, Old Oak Industries.' Mr Doyle took a piece of cheese from his pocket and popped it into his mouth. 'It's amazing what you remember when you least expect it. Why, just the other day I was thinking about penny-farthing bicycles...'

'Mr Doyle,' Jack said.

'Of course.' The detective smiled. 'I recalled the name Darrow originates from the ancient words for "oak tree". It meant that Darrow may have owned the building. I remembered then that a cross-city railway project had been discontinued when new Parliament was built and the line ran under the building.'

Gloria shook her head in admiration. 'What a brain you have, Ignatius,' she said. 'And what about the native man who was guarding Atlantis? What was his name?'

'Etruba,' Jack said. 'He and his brother were the last Atlanteans. Etruba wanted to avoid bloodshed, but Andana was prepared to do anything necessary to keep the city secret.'

'How did they get involved with Darrow's plan?'

'We can't be certain,' Mr Doyle said. 'But they must have heard about the unearthing of the Broken Sun and followed the pieces back to England. They may have realised Darrow was watching the museum. Andana infiltrated Darrow's group, but always had the intention to take back the Broken Sun.

'After Andana was killed, rather than allowing the secrets of New Atlantis to fall into the hands of unbelievers, Etruba destroyed the city. He wanted to destroy the signal that was calling their gods back to Earth.'

'But surely that's just a legend?' Gloria said.

'There may be some truth in it. Jack and Scarlet's description of the gods in the murals at New Atlantis sound remarkably like people in space suits.'

'What?' Jack squawked. 'You mean people from other worlds? Men from Mars?'

'Probably not Mars,' Mr Doyle said. 'Maybe from much further away.'

'I hope they've called off their visit,' Gloria said, taking a sip of tea.

'Unless they're almost here,' Scarlet said, glancing up at the ceiling as if expecting one to pop through.

'Then I'll keep the teapot warm. Just in case.' Gloria ate a cream biscuit. 'And finally, what about Phoebe, Clarice and Professor Clarke?'

'Already planning another expedition,' Mr Doyle said. 'One that is expected to take some time. As the location of New Atlantis has been established, they now want to find a way to excavate the city.'

'That could take years. Decades.'

'Archaeologists are very patient people. And New Atlantis probably still holds many secrets waiting to be recovered from its watery tomb.'

'I expect you will miss them,' Gloria said, her eyes honing in on Mr Doyle. 'Especially Phoebe.'

He raised an eyebrow. 'An invitation has been made for Phoebe to visit at Christmas. It would be nice to see her again.'

A knock came from the outer office.

'Speaking of visitors…' Jack said.

Mr Doyle rose wordlessly and left the room. Gloria leaned close to Jack and Scarlet. 'How is he?' she asked. 'Ignatius seems rather…apprehensive.'

'He's been quieter than usual,' Jack admitted. 'And he hasn't been eating as much cheese.'

Scarlet bit her bottom lip. 'It's not every day a man gets his family back,' she said.

The door to the sitting room opened. Mr Doyle appeared first, followed by a small young boy. Amelia Doyle came next, pushing a wheelchair with Phillip Doyle in it.

Jason Doyle had brown hair and the same dark eyes as Mr Doyle. Amelia, since their first meeting at Harwich, seemed like a different woman. Her smile was still sad, but her eyes were bright and there was colour in her cheeks.

Phillip's eyes were open, but unfocused. He had not spoken since he and the other machine men were recovered from Parliament. The exoskeletons had protected him and his brothers in arms.

'I'll make more tea,' Gloria said.

'No.' Jack held up his hand. 'I'll do that.'

As he made a fresh pot, he wondered what the future would hold for them all. Certainly it would not all be smooth sailing. The damage to Phillip's mind might take years to repair.

Jack returned with the teapot. Scarlet was handing the plate of biscuits around. Amelia had her arm over Phillip's shoulder.

Scarlet looked up at Jack. 'We were just discussing the importance of reading,' she said. 'I was just telling everyone about the Brinkie Buckeridge novels.'

'She does that a lot,' Jack told the group. 'You'll get used to it.'

Jason placed his hand on Mr Doyle's arm. 'May I have another biscuit, please?' he asked.

'Of course, my boy.' The detective looked ten years younger with his family around. Biscuits were offered and accepted. 'Your mother tells me you love to sing?'

'I'm in the church choir.'

Mr Doyle nodded thoughtfully. 'You know,' he said, 'there's a song I used to sing to your father. Would you like to hear it?'

'Yes, please,' the boy said.

'Jason has a very good voice,' Amelia said. 'He's often chosen to sing solo.'

'Really?' Mr Doyle looked delighted. 'Then perhaps we'll sing it together.'

He hummed a few bars to get them started, then began to softly sing.

'*The Minstrel Boy will return we pray. When we hear the news we all will cheer it—*'

He stopped. Another voice, a low whisper, had joined him, and they all turned in astonishment. Phillip Doyle's eyes were still unfocused, but from somewhere deep inside him, from a place that the war and George Darrow had not been able to reach, came the words. Like an echo from a life that was, they signalled a life that could finally be.

'*The Minstrel Boy will return one day*,' Phillip sang. '*Torn perhaps in body, not in spirit.*'